Praise for Avery Flynn's Books:

"Sexy and sassy... Avery Flynn brings it all."—*Carly Phillips, NY Times Bestselling Author*

"This book is so good you won't want to put it down."—*Harlequin Junkie, Enemies on Tap*

"Flynn intertwines fashionistas and fighters in book two of this heavily talked-about series and she'll leave readers breathless by the time they reach the heart-pounding finish."—*4.5 starts Top Pick, RT Book Reviews, This Year's Black*

Flynn knows her sass and sex ... sheer naughty fun!"—*Into the Fire author Amanda Usen, Betting the Billionaire*

"I loved this story."—*Darynda Jones, NY Times Bestselling Author, Jax and the Beanstalk Zombies*

"...Thrilling, funny   passionate and even contains a few tips to keep the fashion police away from your doorstep."—*RT Book Reviews, High-Heeled Wonder*

Dangerous *Flirt*

(Laytons Book Two)

By
Avery Flynn

Visit Avery's website at www.averyflynn.com.

Edited by KC
Formatting by Anessa Books

ISBN: 978-0-9908335-4-3 (D) 978-0-9908335-7-4 (P)
Manufactured in the United States of America

First Edition: 2012 (Seduction Creek)
Revision: May 2015 (Dangerous Flirt)

Dedication

For my family, those by blood and those by luck, you've

made all the difference.

Acknowledgement

A huge high five to Emma Shortt for all she does, I couldn't have done it without you. A hip bump to my critique partners Kerri and Kimfor bringing me back from the edge of crazy too many times to count. the next trip to Mike's for dinner is on me – except for the bar tab because y'all know I'm not a millionaire.

Author Note

Dangerous Flirt was first published in 2012 as Seduction Creek, but has since been revised.

Chapter One

Twenty years ago.

From her spot in the backseat, Beth Martinez held her breath and watched the glowing green numbers. The nine disappeared, replaced by a one and a zero. Ten o'clock. Two hours past her bedtime. A new record.

She shimmied her eight-year-old butt in the seat. The seat belt scratching against her neck tempered her crazy dance moves. In the front seat, her parents yammered on about boring grown-up things, totally clueless about her quiet celebration.

The drive home from Denver had taken longer than usual, thanks to some well-timed whining for dinner. That move had been brilliant. Her papá had frowned at her in the rearview mirror, but her puppy-dog eyes had him pulling into the last Denny's before they crossed the Nebraska state line. The neon-blue lemonade with sprinkles hadn't tasted as good as it looked on TV, but still, Beth couldn't wait to tell everyone at Dry Creek Elementary that she'd tried it.

"Mi'ja, honey, do you have to go to the bathroom?"

Heat burned her cheeks. "Nah, I'm good."

Papá shrugged. "Whatever you say, my favorite daughter."

"I'm your only daughter." She rolled her eyes.

"Why mess with perfection?" her mother piped in and winked at Beth.

Their station wagon passed into the Bighorn Hills, always spooky at night with its sagebrush shadows and coyotes howling from behind the pine trees. Twenty more minutes and they'd be home in Dry Creek, Nebraska, the last town on earth without a Denny's.

No way would she get in bed before ten-thirty. Now that would be beyond record breaking. Even her best friend Claire's brother, Hank, had to be in bed before then and he was fourteen.

Up later than a teenager. Awesome.

Their car rounded the curve and her body pulled to the left. Light flooded the interior and Beth's hand flew to her eyes, blocking out the brightness.

"What the hell," her father grumbled. "This asshole is all over the road."

Beth went on alert. José Martinez never cussed. She craned her neck around her mother's seat to get a better look, wondering what had gotten her father so mad.

A big, square car crossed from one side of the road to the other as it headed right for them.

The blue lemonade gurgled in her stomach when she looked out the window. On one side, sagebrush and prickly pine trees covered the hilly landscape. On the other, the Bighorn Hills sloped down toward the valley and Dry Creek's streetlights. Forget about not having a Denny's, she wanted to be home. Now.

"Mamá!"

"It's okay, honey. We'll just pull over to the side a bit and give that car plenty of room to pass." Her mother twisted and re-twisted a strand of thick brown hair around her finger.

The car swerved to the far side of the road before jerking back into the center of the highway.

Her father moved their station wagon to the opposite side, close to the drop off. Gravel spit up from beneath the tires.

"Are we going to be all right?"

"Sure, mi'ja, nothing to worry about." Her father's fingers curled so tightly around the steering wheel that his brown knuckles had paled in the dashboard's glow.

The car drifted again and then drove to the opposite side of the highway before it popped back in their direction as if snapped by a rubber band.

"Hold on everyone!" her father yelled. The screech of metal tearing against metal drowned out any other words as the sedan plowed into them.

Their station wagon sailed off the highway and through the trees, picking up speed as it charged downward. It slammed into something big and somersaulted through the air.

Beth's body floated up from her seat, the seatbelt biting into the soft skin at the base of her neck. Her head whipped back and forth as the station wagon flipped over and over.

With nothing holding them secure, her parents tumbled around the interior, their bodies slamming against the doors, windows and the ceiling. Over and under, around and about, the station wagon crashed through the trees until it landed with a thunk upside down.

The world swam in front of her and Beth puked bright-blue vomit that landed with a splash on the ceiling. The safety belt cut into her waist and chest, keeping her in her seat while her body hung upside down.

Her long brown hair, wet and sticky from the puke, clung to her face like a curtain, blocking her view of the front seat. "Mamá! Papá?" Her cries were weak compared to the deafening roar of blood rushing through her ears.

No answer.

Clenching her eyes shut, Beth tried to block out the world. She must have fallen asleep in the car and this was a nightmare. Determined to make it true, she counted to ten, fully prepared to open her eyes and see her parents talking in the front seat as if nothing had happened. Because nothing *had* happened. Nothing.

One.

Two.

Three.

They'd be talking about abuelito's retirement party.

Four.

Five.

Six.

Mamá would laugh at something Papá said and then lean across the seat to kiss him on the cheek.

Seven.

Eight.

Nine.

Papá would say "good morning, mi'ja", even though it was ten o'clock at night.

Ten.

Beth didn't even have to open her eyes to know something had happened. Something awful.

A wet gasping sound came from the front seat.

She opened her eyes and parted her hair, pushing it back out of her face.

First, she saw the empty spot where her father had sat behind the steering wheel.

Next, the hole in the windshield, big enough for a man to fall out of and disappear forever.

Finally, her mother's long brown hair tangled around her once pretty and now bruised and bloodied face. Her body lay twisted on the station wagon's ceiling, but her face looked up, her brown eyes unfocused.

"Maaaaaaaammmmmmmááááááá!"

One of her mother's eyes twitched, but nothing else moved. Her mouth gaped open as she wheezed in a desperate breath and exhaled a wet one.

Beth slapped at the seatbelt, trying to unlock it, straining against the nylon. "Mamá, help. I can't get to you."

A single tear slid from her mother's eye, the droplet tracing its way across the bruise reddening her cheekbone.

Papá had disappeared.

Mamá lay unmoving.

Beth couldn't escape, couldn't help, couldn't do anything.

Terror blacked out everything. She kicked her legs until one of her Keds flew off. She beat the window with a fist and thrashed about. Exhausted after only minutes, Beth's harsh breathing filled the car.

Only when her panting slowed did she realize it had been the only sound in the car.

As if on its own power, her gaze landed on her mother's still figure. "Mamá."

Her mother wouldn't answer ever again. Guilt twisted around her heart and squeezed.

All because of her.

If she hadn't whined, they wouldn't have stopped for dinner. Her family would be home. She'd be asleep in her bed. They never would have seen the other car. None of this would have happened if she hadn't been so selfish.

It was all her fault.

Chapter Two

Today.

*H*ank Layton surveyed the late dinner crowd at Juanita's, munching away on enchiladas and plates loaded with puffed-up tortilla chips covered in frijoles, melted cheese, guacamole and jalapeños. His stomach growled as if he hadn't eaten in a year.

"Hey ya, sheriff. Just you today?" The Juanita of Juanita's strode up to him armed with a menu he knew by heart.

"Just me. Can you put me in the back room?"

"Trying to avoid the ladies elbowing each other out of line to be the next Mrs. Layton?"

"Not quite." He lowered his voice. "It's my mom."

"What is it this time?" she asked.

"Founders Day is coming up–"

"Got you working overtime, huh?"

"The woman is a slave driver and she sees it as the perfect opportunity to grill me about grandkids."

Juanita shook her head knowingly. "For most people, I'd say what's wrong with a mama who's concerned with her children, but for you, I say I have the perfect table. Come on."

He followed her through the cramped dining area, past the Mexican flag depicted in neon light and into an area that was more of a large alcove than a separate room. She handed him a menu and waved him in before scurrying to the kitchen, presumably for chips and salsa.

The back room held four two-person tables. A woman occupied one.

Beth Martinez sat with her back to him with her I'm-a-serious-lawyer jacket slung haphazardly over the back of the chair. The strands of her normally silky-smooth, long brown hair stuck up at odd angles. She sighed and slouched lower in her seat.

He'd known Beth since she and his little sister Claire became Girl Scouts together in second grade, but this was the first time he'd ever seen her looking so...lost. The Mexican-themed red and yellow lamps put a spotlight on the faint tremble of Beth's shoulders. All huddled up and turned away, her body language said "leave me alone", but he couldn't. Something more than common decency, he didn't know what, pushed him toward her table.

"Hey there."

Her head shot up. Even with the barrier of her glasses, he could tell she'd been crying. She took a quick swipe at a cheek with the back of her hand.

"Mind if I join you? I hate eating by myself." He turned up the charm wattage on his smile when she eyed the exit. "Come on, I'll buy your dinner and we'll call it even from all the times I stole your Ring Dings when you and Claire had sleepovers."

One side of her mouth curled upward. "I always wondered which one of you brothers stole them."

He held up his right hand. "Guilty as charged. So I'll make it up." He sat down in the free chair at her table.

This time her smile involved her whole mouth. "Have a seat."

Eyeing her still closed menu, he settled back against the seat. "Good, you haven't ordered yet. How hungry are you? Because I'm starving."

As if on cue, her stomach growled. "Famished."

"Are you woman enough for the Double Date?" He laughed when she gave him the side eye. "On the menu."

She flipped open her menu, traced a finger down the list of entrees, paused for a moment and arched her eyebrows. "Three chimichangas, four enchiladas, a double order of rice and beans and sopapillas for dessert. Are you kidding?"

"Come on, live life on the wild side."

"You'd have to roll me out of here afterward."

Hank looked, really looked, at Beth. Even though she sat, he knew her body was long and lean, with muscular thighs and an ass you could play quarters on. Shit, he'd known that since coming home after a four-year, post-college stint in the Marines. She'd been twenty years old with hair down to her waist and the sweetest little strut he'd ever seen. The woman had been—and still was—a knockout. But there was something more to her now than when she was barely legal, some extra air of...hell, he couldn't describe it, but it sure made his dick sit up and take notice.

"I doubt that, you're looking fine." His gaze roamed her light brown skin, locking in on the small patch of lace peeking out from the scoop-necked shirt she'd been tugging on. "More than fine, really."

"Uh...thanks." She fidgeted with her menu then stuffed her hands in her lap.

Oh hell. What was he doing? This was his little sister's best friend, practically a second sister since she'd spent so much time at their house while growing up. Beth was not a possible fuck buddy, which was all he wanted or needed.

Damn straight. The ink on his divorce papers had only been dry for eight months. Relationships were not on his radar right now, which meant Beth inhabited a no-fucking zone.

An awkward silence descended while he tried to figure out how to disengage his foot from his big mouth. Luckily, the arrival of their waiter with the chips and salsa released the tension.

"So are you ready to order?" The waiter held his pen at the ready.

"Yeah, we'll have the Double Date. I have a Dos Equis. Do you want a beer?"

"No." She shook her head. "I'm not really a drinker. I'll take a Pepsi."

The waiter scribbled down their order and hustled back to the kitchen. Hank went back to wondering how to fill the silence.

જ∙જ∙જ

He didn't mean anything by it. It's just the way he is. Hank Layton flirts the way normal human beings breathe.

Beth had been there. Almost done that. Wasn't going back for more.

Okay. That helped to bring her heart rate back to normal, if you considered cheetah-speed normal. Of course, after the day she'd had, it was no wonder her reactions were out of whack. She took a drink of ice-cold water, watching Hank over the top of her glass, and almost dropped it. He was staring right at her. Her stomach fluttered—which was better than the twisted anxiety tying her guts up in knots since this morning because of the latest in a string of threatening calls.

This feeling was all about Hank, all six feet, three inches of him. She'd memorized that stat his first year of playing quarterback for the University of Nebraska. She'd tacked the page with his picture and stats from a football program to the back of her closet in high school. She would have taped it to the ceiling above her bed, but couldn't begin to think of a way to explain that one to her abuelita. Or Claire, who would have reminded her that Hank was her bossy oldest brother with the world's meanest girlfriend. The one who had become his wife and, now, his ex-wife.

A pair of dark jeans encased his long legs, loose enough to be casual and tight enough to cling to the ass she lusted after despite knowing she shouldn't. An untucked Nebraska football T-shirt covered his wide shoulders and hid the washboard abs that haunted the restless nights she spent alone in bed, unable to sleep.

"So," Hank drawled. "How's the world treating you today?"

Honestly? Like a redheaded stepchild. "I'll live."

"That's always good news." He smirked. "Rough day?"

"No doubt about it. You?"

"Every day since mom roped me into that Founder's Day fiasco is a mess. It's her second favorite topic since she and dad moved back permanently to Dry Creek."

The waiter delivered their drinks.

Hank took a long pull from the beer bottle. "I have a proposition to make. Let's not talk about our day, the crazy people around us or any other general bitching."

"I'm game."

"What should we talk about?"

"The weather?"

He rolled his eyes. "Lame."

"Politics?"

"Hell no. I'm trying to eat here." He popped a chip heavy with salsa into his mouth.

"Okay, so you pick."

"Sex." The word came out in a single-syllable dare.

The frisson of attraction that normally buzzed in the background whenever she was near Hank moved front and center. It reached out, making her nipples tingle. "I don't—"

"No specifics," he interrupted. "Just general factoids. I'll start. Women who work out have more orgasms than those who don't."

"How do you know that?"

"You should know that already, you're at the gym what, three times a week?"

"Five," she squeaked out.

The green in his hazel eyes darkened and he stared at her expectantly.

Her breath caught. Damn, she couldn't think over the dirty movie playing in her head at the moment. But the longer she stayed silent, the greener his eyes turned and the wetter her panties became. Desperate, her brain finally stumbled upon a factoid.

"The most popular flavor of edible underwear is cherry. Totally true, I read it in *Cosmo*."

"Cherry's always been a favorite flavor of mine."

When did her bra get so tight? It had fit perfectly this morning. Now the lace cups scratched against her hard nipples with enough friction to annoy but not enough to ease the lust turning her brain to mush.

"Got one." He chuckled softly. "Vegetarians like to give blow jobs more than meat eaters."

The waiter picked that moment to arrive at their table with a tray loaded down with Mexican food. He acted as if he hadn't heard anything, but the tips of his ears were pink. Keeping his eyes glued to the table, he made fast work of unloading the food, the dishes clanking on the wood table, then sped back into the main dining room.

They busied themselves with filling their plates from the family-style serving dishes. More relaxed than she'd been in months, she snagged an enchilada, cut a chimichanga in half and scooped rice onto her plate. She savored the first bite of cheese and onion wrapped in a handmade corn tortilla. Not as good as abuelita's, but awful close. Next, a bite of beef chimichanga. The deep-fried shell snapped under her fork as she cut off a piece, making sure to get some guacamole with it. The seasoned beef revitalized her taste buds. She felt more herself with every second that passed.

"It's not true, you know," she said before taking a second bite of chimichanga.

"What's that?"

"About blow jobs. Carnivores love oral sex."

Hank's cock caught her meaning a full five seconds before his brain and he choked on his enchilada.

His eyes watered as he reached for his beer. All the while, she ate her chimichanga like nothing had happened, as if she hadn't just given him a month's worth of wank-off material.

She blinked her big brown eyes at him, an innocent look on her face. "You okay?"

No. Absolutely not. "Affirmative," he managed to sputter.

Entranced, he watched as she did some sort of girl trick where she flicked her head and all of that luscious, shoulder-length brown hair fell into place. God, what he'd give to bury his fingers in that silk while she went down on him. His mouth went dry. He didn't think it was possible, but he got harder.

Let's talk about sex. What a boneheaded idea that had been.

"The workout thing?" She paused to take a drink of her Pepsi. "I can confirm that."

Fuck.

Chapter Three

$\mathcal{B}$eth smoothed down her white skirt, as if by doing so, she could soothe the lust buzzing inside her like she had swallowed a beehive. It had been like this every day for the past three weeks since her dinner with Hank. And at night? Her fantasies would make porn stars blush.

What had she been thinking that night at dinner? Just remembering her quip about carnivores had heat steaming her skin. Flirting with Hank wasn't just swimming out of her depth, it equated to treading water in shark-infested ocean with a twenty-pound weight tied to her toes. Not a good idea.

And yet, here she was in Claire's living room, toasting her best friend's soon-to-be-rebuilt Harvest Bistro while denying her secret hope that Hank would throw her over his shoulder, sneak her away and ravage her until her body turned to Jell-O.

"Guess what I just heard." Claire nudged Beth with an elbow.

She looked down at her best friend. Claire had every right to bask. Everything in her life had gotten back on track and as a bonus, she had Jake to share it with. It had taken a psycho killer and one completely twisted family to bring the two of them together, but they'd managed to turn all that ugly into something beautiful.

"Spill it."

Claire hooked her arm through Beth's elbow and tugged her to one of the few unoccupied spots in the living room. "That troll of an ex-wife of Hank's, Amanda, used her alimony payments as collateral in some investment scheme tied to the new casino."

"What kind of scheme?"

"Well, you know how the Lakota Tribe announced yesterday the casino entrance would be on Highway Five?"

"Uh-huh."

"She was part of the group that bought Fred Nathan's farm, which butts up against the reservation. That bitch is going to make a mint using Hank's money. Why he even agreed to alimony, I'll never know. The woman blackmailed him with the promise of babies for most of their marriage."

Beth's stomach dropped.

Her nonexistent womb clenched. Veterans who lost limbs in war reported feeling their phantom limbs decades after it had been blown to bits. Why shouldn't she feel the uterus she'd lost after her doctor had found a fibroid tumor four months ago?

For the millionth time, she almost told Claire about the outpatient laser surgery, but couldn't. Saying it out loud would make it real. And after losing the rest of her family already, Beth couldn't bear to admit she'd lost the future family she hadn't realized she wanted until it was too late.

"What? I didn't know he wanted kids."

"Oh yeah. Mr. Mom, that's Hank. But don't tell my mom. She's on his case enough as it is." Claire paused as a trio of women walked by. "When he told me that Amanda even faked a pregnancy to keep him from leaving at the end? What a complete bitch. No wonder he's dating half the county."

Beth shoved her secret into a dark room in her mind and added one more line to the seemingly endless list of reasons why Hank wasn't for her. "Wow."

Fire practically blazed from the ends of Claire's red hair. "Exactly." She pivoted, the look on her face the same as the time she'd talked Beth into climbing the fence around the country club's pool and going skinny dipping with Mike Hanson and Steve Gerke. "You should date Hank."

"No."

"Hear me out. You have the same sense of humor. You're both smart. You've had a crush on him for forever." She rolled her eyes. "Don't give me that look. Of course I know. And, you two could get married so we'd be sisters!"

Stall, Beth. Stall. "Why is it people who are in a relationship suddenly want everyone to join them?"

"Don't try to change the subject."

Chalk one up to the best friend bullshit detector. "I don't want to date Hank."

"Why not? Give me one good reason."

"You know why not."

"Are you talking about what happened between you two a million years ago? Really? Ancient history. Come up with a better reason or I'm breaking out my matchmaking skills."

Beth gulped, her brain fizzling under the pressure. She wouldn't risk losing Claire and the whole Layton clan, who'd practically adopted her, if a roll in the hay with Hank turned into heartbreak and ugliness. And if it did work out, she'd be forcing him to give up having kids. She wouldn't accept either option.

She latched on to the only part of the truth she could say out loud. "He's your brother."

"So?"

"If things went wrong, and you know it would end badly, it could make things awkward between us."

Claire snaked an arm around Beth's much higher waist and gave her a quick hug. "Oh, Beth. There's not a damn thing in this world that could submarine us."

"Still..."

"Fine. I'll keep my big mouth shut," she huffed. "But if I end up with another bitch for a sister-in-law, I will hold it against you forever."

୧ଡ଼୧ଡ଼୧ଡ଼

Hank couldn't look away from Beth's glossy, red lips. Even from across the living room, the sight of those full lips touching the rim of her wine glass as she sipped the white liquid had him hooked. He needed to get her alone.

"Dude, I think you're drooling. Not cool." His youngest brother, Chris, held a small mountain of BBQ chips in one hand and sucked the reddish orange powder off the fingers of his other.

"Thanks, Miss Manners, what would I do without you?"

Chris rolled his eyes. "It's Beth. Claire'd kick your ass."

"What makes you think she'd need to?"

His brother snorted and shoved the mound of chips into his mouth. After crunching them into submission, he took a swig of beer. "Whatever." He let out a low whistle. "Break Beth's heart and Claire will take you apart bone by bone."

"Butt out."

Something had happened at Juanita's. She'd staked a claim in his subconscious, the smell of her vanilla perfume had taken up residence in his nostrils, and the look in her eye when she'd taunted him with that line about carnivores and blow jobs haunted him every night.

Chris rammed an elbow into his ribs. "Get ahold of yourself, you're embarrassing me."

"I won't break Beth's heart."

Because right now she was stomping all over his, ignoring his calls and avoiding him like the plague. Even at the party, she shimmied away anytime he came within ten feet.

Enough of being a wuss. He'd led the University of Nebraska to the BCS championship. If he could take on a defensive line packed with three-hundred pounders, what challenge did one amazingly hot woman pose? Sufficiently psyched, he zeroed in on Beth's location and marched forward.

Like a bunny sensing danger, she spotted him while he still had half the room to go. She slid her fingers through her silky brown hair and her gaze flicked from one side of the crowded room to the other, everywhere but on him.

A third of the way there, his cock twitched in recognition of her being near. His fingers itched to strip the white frilly dress away from her brown skin and lick every inch he exposed.

His quarry clutched at the silver chain around her slim neck that dipped between her pert tits and beneath her dress. She couldn't look away from him now. Her lips parted slightly and her pink tongue darted out, licking her bottom lip.

Two steps and he'd be within touching distance.

The worry lines smoothed from her forehead.

His gut lurched.

Damn, she'd figured a way out. Again.

"Hank, there you are," she greeted him as if she had no idea of all the things he'd like to do to her delectable body. "Sarah Jane was just telling me about her latest scrapbooking project. It's fascinating. I'm sure she could give you some tips for the Layton family tree your mom has you putting together. Why don't you two chat while I circle to make sure everyone has a drink."

Whippet quick, she dashed away, leaving him no choice but to listen to a half-hour dissertation about the importance of archival-quality paper.

Oh, she was good, but he had time on his side.

Let the hunt begin.

It took Hank exactly fifty-three minutes to get Beth alone. Actually, he stumbled upon her in the hallway completely by accident, but that's not how he'd tell the story years from now.

She stared at a Layton family photo with intensity and a hint of something else that made him pause before his gaze traveled down her long, lean body to the flimsy white heels strapped to her feet. Her dress covered her legs down to her knees, but he had memorized the curve of her thighs years ago.

"I was wondering how long it would take you."

So tangled up in observation, her words caught him completely off guard. Hell, he needed to work on his stealth skills. "You were timing me?"

"Yep." She turned, pushed her glasses up her nose and crossed her arms. "You unwound yourself from Sarah Jane Hunihan with record speed."

Everything about her stance said stay away, except for her slight smile and the undeniable interest twinkling in her brown eyes that her black-rimmed glasses couldn't hide. Taking a chance, he closed the distance between them, stopping outside of an arm's reach. He didn't trust himself not to brush the long strand of black hair away from her high cheekbone.

"How long are we going to play this game?"

Her warm brown skin tinged pink at her cheeks. "What game?"

Fuck it. Another step closer and he pushed the rebellious strand back. The air sizzled around them. "The one where I chase and you run."

A dozen emotions crossed her face in quick succession and her long fingers picked at one of the frills on her neckline. Her lips parted and he zoned in on her sweet mouth, hypnotized by its luscious promise. Electricity sparked between them stronger than a lightning bolt and for a second he thought he'd won her over. Then, the lust in her eyes retreated behind some inner wall.

"Until you realize the ending isn't the one you want."

"What ending is that?"

"I won't be one more number for you to call on Saturday night." Her breathy voice teased him, making his jeans fit more snugly than they had five minutes ago.

"What makes you think that's what I want from you?"

27

"It's all you've wanted from any woman since your divorce."

"But those women aren't you." He traced a finger down her smooth cheek. "There's something about you that has me wanting more. A lot more."

She quirked a thin eyebrow at him. "Uh-huh."

Time for the direct approach. "Come out with me."

"No."

"Why?"

"Because you're my best friend's brother."

Not the response he'd expected. "What does that have to do with anything?"

Her silence and the way her gaze slid to the left screamed out how much of a bullshit excuse it was. Damn, Beth would be the death of him. She wanted him. He wanted her. What the hell was the problem?

"I need to get back to the party." She circled around him.

Oh, hell no.

He stopped her with a light touch on her hip.

She let out the smallest of sighs, but to his ears it sounded as loud as a tornado plowing through a trailer park.

Pulling her closer, he inhaled her vanilla scent. "When you're ready to stop lying to me and tell me what this is really about, I will be here to listen. But this," he lowered his head, "is real."

Brushing his lips against hers, his body responded the moment she relaxed into his arms. She tasted of wine and sweetness and unfulfilled promise. As she softened against him, everything about him hardened. He spread his fingers wide on her round hip, the tips grazing her firm ass, and pulled her to him. She rubbed against his fast-hardening cock and he almost lost it right then and there.

Beth pushed him away. Breathing hard, her eyes dark with passion. Without saying a word, she slipped through his fingers and hurried down the hall.

Alone in the hallway, Hank fought to calm his hammering heart and bring his body back under control. But he wasn't likely to accomplish either until he found a way to win over Beth Martinez.

అల్లల్ల

A week later, he still hadn't come up with a decent plan. Sure, kidnapping her and carrying her off to a remote cabin had crossed his mind, but him being the Dry Creek County sheriff kind of negated actual law-breaking.

"Stop lollygagging and bring me that box of mementoes down from the attic."

Ah, the sweet dulcet tones of his mother, Glenda, on a Founder's Day preparation binge. A few more hours as the dutiful eldest son, then it was Friday poker night at Mike's, and finally out to Vegas on the first flight on Monday to meet his brothers for the traditional Layton poker trip. Playing cards always helped him think. He'd figure out how to get on Beth's good side while staring at a full house.

"Are you taking a nap up there? Get a move on."

Gritting his teeth, he grabbed the box marked "Rebecca's Bounty" in red marker and hefted it down the stairs. "Where do you want it?"

"Over on the table by the family tree would be perfect. Thanks."

He nudged a portrait of his great-great-grandmother Emma Davenport a few inches to the left and lowered the box onto the oak table. "What's in this thing anyway?"

His mother appeared out of the kitchen dressed in jeans and a sparkly T-shirt. She carried a bowl and two spoons. "That is your great-great." She paused and scrunched up her nose. "Oh, I'm not sure how many greats it is, but it's your great-grandmother's belongings. Come sit down and help me eat this, I accidentally got too much."

She moved the family Bible to the center of the table and set down the bowl. Three gigantic scoops of chocolate ice cream complete with whipped cream and sprinkles filled the speckled blue bowl. His favorite. That meant only one thing—trouble ahead. Well, at least he'd get grilled on a full stomach.

"I thought Uncle Harlan lost Rebecca's diary in a poker game a few years back." He dug into the sundae.

"Oh that man. He's lucky he still gets invited to Thanksgiving dinner." She pursed her lips. "The treasure hunters only valued her diary, but the historical society is putting together a display of her other belongings as part of the Founder's Day celebration."

"They're going Layton crazy, are they?"

"Our family did help settle Dry Creek. Didn't I raise you to be proud of your legacy?"

The hairs on the back of his neck pricked up. Damn, half the ice cream still sat melting in the bowl, but he'd started Glenda down the wrong path and there was no going back.

"And when are you going to find a nice girl to settle down with and have kids to build upon that legacy?"

Soon. Not that he could tell his mother that.

"What happened to make my children so marriage-averse?" She sighed melodramatically. "You're not getting any younger you know."

"Maybe after Amanda, I'm not so keen on getting married again."

Glenda harrumphed. "That girl? She was never the right one for you. I must have told you after every one of the dozen break ups you had starting in high school. But did you listen? Nope. I'm just your mother. What would I know?"

"Or it could be that I have someone in mind, but she doesn't want anything to do with me."

She looked up, aghast. "Who wouldn't love you?"

"Careful, Mom, you're starting to sound like you've gone soft and mushy."

"Enough of that smart mouth, mister." She nailed him to his seat with her best mama bear look. "That ex-wife of yours is a real piece of work. I'd like to use other words for her, but your father put up a swear jar in the kitchen last week. I've already deposited three dollars." Speculation twinkled in her dark-brown eyes. "How about Beth Martinez? She's such a nice girl. You've known each other forever. Why don't you ask her out?"

Like a man trying to disarm a ticking time bomb, he weighed his options, both of which were ugly. Cutting the green wire meant keeping his mom in the dark. When she did find out—and she would, being Dry Creek's biggest gossip—she'd hang him out to dry. Snipping the blue wire equaled spilling the beans and begging her not to get involved. Like that would ever happen.

"Mom—"

"I know, I know, butt out. The way you kids act you'd think I was always in your business."

Opting for silence being the better option, Hank waited her out. It took all of three breaths.

"Fine, fine. I won't interfere." She stood and scooped up the bowl of half-eaten ice cream from the table. "Now, enough lounging about. There are six more boxes I need down from the attic."

He dropped a kiss on the top of his mother's head. "Will do."

Chapter Four

The rich aroma of fresh-ground coffee at Get Buzzed always transported Beth to her happy place. Fruity, tropical drinks with paper umbrellas had nothing on a good cup of joe...or latte...or mocha...or, well, anything hot and caffeinated. And today, she needed it.

Inhaling the heady scent, she willed contentment to seep into her bones. Like she had since her hysterectomy, which came right on the heels of the six-month anniversary of her abuelita's passing, she'd stayed up half the night trying to process what a life without the possibility of a future family would be like.

This morning she woke up determined to move forward. There wasn't a damn thing she could do about the hysterectomy. It was done. She would push past the pain and plunge back into her normal routine. Was it the best way to deal with grief? Probably not, but it was the only way she knew how.

Determined to make this Saturday morning perfect, no matter what, she bounced out of bed as soon as her alarm clock beeped. First, a few hours with the newspaper and her coffee, the sweet nectar of the gods. Second, off to the gym, where she'd change into workout gear and go one-on-one with the boxing bag. Third, devouring an iced cinnamon roll while reviewing the pro bono wills she had drawn up for a handful of nursing home residents.

But first thing first. Unscrewing the top of her mug, she stepped up to the counter.

"Next," the barista called out.

Beth handed over her mug and blew on her hands, chilled from the crisp late October air, then pulled out the emergency twenty dollar bill she kept in her gym bag. "Caramel mocha with a double shot of espresso please."

"One regular it is." The woman scribbled her order on the mug with a dry-erase marker and handed it to a teenager manning the espresso machine.

Beth moseyed down to the pickup end of the counter, her attention fixated on the newest bunch of bee-themed coffee mugs for sale. Fat bumblebees circled flowers with coffee bean centers on a bright yellow ceramic cup. Two worker bees clinked coffee mugs on a blue to-go cup. She picked up one with tiny bees spelling out, "Get Buzzed in Dry Creek, Nebraska", for closer inspection.

"Caramel mocha double espresso ready." A boy with boredom-glazed eyes handed over her drink.

"Thank you." The coffee's warmth seeped into her palm. Heaven. The chocolate scent jolted her system into working order. Everything would be better now.

She blew away the steam and screwed on the lid, then slung her gym bag over her shoulder. As she swerved through the maze of tiny tables crowding the floor between the counter and the door, her cell vibrated against her butt. Shrugging her stuffed gym bag higher up on her shoulder, she grabbed her phone out of her back pocket.

"Hello?"

"Um...Ms. Martin..."

Beth sighed and pushed open the heavy glass door with her hip. "Martinez." The cold wind blasted her, sending a chill down her spine.

"Yeah, Ms. Martinez. I'm Deputy Schnell with the Council County Sheriff's Office. Can you meet me at your grandparents' home? Seems it's been broken into."

৯৯৯

Fifteen minutes and twenty miles later, Beth stalked out of the tiny living room in her dead grandparents' vacant home. Technically it was her house now, but she couldn't think of it that way.

She traced the curse words spray painted in red on the foyer walls. Most were in English, but centered on the oak front door in large, block capital letters and underlined with a bold swoosh was the word *puta*.

Nice try, but she'd been called a lot worse. Whoever had done this had crossed a line they shouldn't have.

Looked like the nasty calls and threatening texts had been only the beginning. The assholes had upped the ante. Her tormentor had promised she'd regret her decision not to sell. He'd sorely misjudged her reaction to this because it wasn't regret making her blood boil.

Something crunched under her favorite cherry-red cowboy boots as she marched across the hall. She stepped sideways and glanced down at the remains of a broken window pane under her sole before taking stock of the damage in the dining room. Where once photos of her grandfather's retirement party, her parents' wedding pictures and her own Quinceañera portrait had hung, fist-sized holes dotted the pale-yellow walls like Swiss cheese. Stomach clenching, her hand reflexively went to her abdomen as if she and not the wall had been punched.

"Uh, Ms. Martin."

She took a steadying sip of coffee, then said, "Martinez."

"No ma'am, my name is Schnell."

She spun around and eyeballed the rail-thin deputy standing in the living room. Is this what law enforcement had come to in rural Western Nebraska? My God, they hadn't just scraped the bottom of the barrel with this guy. No. They'd broken through it, dug around in the muck underneath, pulled up this fine specimen and slapped a uniform on him.

"My *name* is Martinez," she rolled the R and emphasized the Z.

His pale-green eyes bulged and his Adam's apple bobbed convulsively. "Apologies, ma'am, but this was just kids who did this. Sheriff Wilcox said he was sure of it as soon as I told him about the damage." He nodded as if that settled everything.

He continued to chatter, but she listened with half an ear and walked back into the living room. Broken beer bottles and fast-food wrappers littered the thick carpet. If her beloved abuelita had lived long enough to see her pin-neat living room with its daisy wallpaper turned into a trash dump, she would have rained down misery on the litterbug.

Schnell shifted his slight weight from side to side and clutched his hat. "Drunk people...uh...kids...uh...teenagers," he mumbled. His gaze turned toward the large yellow stain on the living room carpet that reeked of ammonia. "It's the only, uh, explanation."

Bullshit.

Beth took another fortifying gulp of coffee. Its heat flowed over her tongue and down her throat, distracting her from her initial impulse to rip the deputy a new one. Not the best plan of action. She was an estate attorney, for God's sake; you couldn't get any more staid than that. She needed to calm down and think logically. Unable to hazard a guess about whether the freckle-faced deputy, who looked all of twelve, was dim or corrupt, she counted to twenty.

"And what about the threatening phone calls telling me my life would go to hell if I didn't sell? Were those from bored kids too, Deputy Schnell?"

His eyes went wide, but he didn't utter a word. Pulling at his loose shirt collar, he gulped hard, as if he'd swallowed one of the slimy frogs from the pond out back.

Heavy footsteps thunked up the front steps, followed by a quick rapping on the open door.

"Heard there was some trouble in the neighborhood and I figured I'd poke my head in to see if I could help." Council County Sheriff Roger Wilcox stood in the doorway, his soft belly protruding over the belt of his uniform pants. A smile curled his lips, barely visible under his gray handlebar mustache.

Just perfect.

For the past two months he'd disregarded her complaints about her neighbors feeling forced to sell and the escalating threats against her. Sure, he'd promised to look into it, but never took any action.

Low priority, he'd claimed. So she'd stewed and tried to dig up any information she could find on the mystery buyer. She'd been tempted to tell Hank, see if he would talk to Wilcox sheriff to sheriff, but her grandparents' house was outside of Hank's Dry Creek County jurisdiction and the last thing she wanted to do was drag him into a turf battle with a neighboring sheriff.

Sweeping her hands across the air to encompass the vandalism, she nodded at the sheriff. "Yep. Seems like someone is trying to send me a message."

He sauntered into the living room and all but ignored his inept deputy fidgeting in the middle of the room. Hands clasped behind his back, the sheriff strolled around the perimeter, stopping here and there to kick at a bottle or brush his fingertips across the red paint.

"Message, eh?" Wilcox faced her. Rubbing his chin, he eyed her for a moment. "I don't know about that. Looks like the handiwork of teenagers to me."

"That's what I told her, sir," the deputy piped in, sending an I-told-you-so look Beth's way.

Wilcox rocked back and forth on his feet. "Good, Schnell." He flashed her an ingratiating smile. "A bright light within our ranks, this one is, which is why I'm assigning him as the lead investigator on your case. If anyone can find the hooligans who did this, it'll be Schnell."

The tips of the deputy's ears reddened and he straightened to his full height of about five feet, seven inches. "Thank you, sir. I'll make you proud."

"And do you have much investigative experience, Deputy Schnell?"

"Everyone has to start somewhere." He scowled.

"And are you going to start with the person snatching up everybody's land? The bully who pushed, prodded and harassed the families living between the county line and the Lakota Reservation?"

"Now, now, young lady, you've expressed your concerns to me before." Wilcox's eyes hardened but the plastic smile remained. "There is nothing to that but rumors and innuendo. The calls and texts you've reported don't say anything about an orchestrated plot to buy up land. As a law enforcement officer, I'm obligated to stick to the facts."

Crossing her arms, she faced off against the sheriff. "And what facts are those?"

He nudged a burger wrapper with the tip of his brown shoe, shined to a high polish. "Why, that the person who did this likes greasy food and cheap beer. That doesn't sound like some high-flying, big-money developer, does it?"

The heat in Beth's flush of indignation would have made dry brush burst into flame, but she kept her mouth shut. She'd played this game with Wilcox several times already. It always turned out the same. He patronized her. She antagonized him. They both stalked off unsatisfied and steaming.

If the stakes had been any lower, Beth would have walked away from the frustration of dealing with an asshole like Wilcox. But the truth was she couldn't. Someone was strong-arming people to sell. Poor Sarah Jane Hunihan finally sold after panic attacks sent her to the emergency room over in Dry Creek. As the last holdout, Beth would be damned if she'd give up the house her grandfather had built with his bare hands for a fistful of cash.

Despite the wreckage around her, she could still see the home where she'd come to live as a newly orphaned eight-year-old girl. Now her grandparents had passed on, leaving her this house. It was the last link to her family, her history, her heritage.

There were no diamonds hanging from her family tree. No Bible handed down from generation to generation. When her grandparents had come here, they'd left Mexico with only what they'd carried in a little suitcase as they followed the crops north. They'd eked out an existence, scrimped and saved to make a better life for their son, José, and later for her. Now there would be no future Martinez generations. How could she sell when this house was all she had left for family?

"I take your silence to mean that you are finally seeing the light." Wilcox swiped away an invisible piece of lint from his brown shirt.

"I wouldn't say that, sheriff." Beth kept her voice low and steady. "So what do you recommend I do to discourage these vandals?" She made air quotes with her fingers.

The smile on Wilcox's face transformed to a mere baring of his wide-spread teeth, and he slapped his brown hat onto his bald head. "My recommendation, Señorita Martinez?" He drew out her last name as he sneered. "Why, I'd recommend selling."

Angry heat spiraled through her body. "I'm sure you would, sheriff, but I'll be damned before I take your advice. Now, since there's nothing you two are really going to do to find who's behind this, I guess I'll have to do it on my own."

"So you're going to do his job?" Wilcox shook his head and twisted his lips into a cruel snarl. "See,

Schnell, this is the problem with our immigration laws. These people come in and start taking jobs away from hard-working Americans." He paused, rubbed a fleshy hand across his large belly before shrugging his shoulders. "But on the other hand, at least this one isn't lazy."

"You piece of shit." The words shot out of her mouth.

Any semblance of civility evaporated from Wilcox's face. His eyes narrowed and he stomped over until his breath fogged up her glasses. "Watch your mouth. You're not under the Dry Creek County sheriff's protection out here."

Beth whipped off her narrow glasses and cleaned them on her black sweater. "I can take care of myself."

He settled his hat back on his head. "You'd better hope so, señorita. You'd better hope so."

"Is that a warning?"

The big man strolled toward the front door, his deputy trailing behind like a puppy. "Nope. I already told you, I deal in facts."

The men hustled out of the house without looking back. Schnell slid easily into his cruiser. Wilcox's car dipped low when he settled his bulk behind the wheel. A second later, dust filled the air as their vehicles spit out gravel and dirt on their way down the driveway and onto Highway 28.

Out of habit, Beth locked the front door. No amount of begging and pleading had convinced the alarm company to come any earlier than next Friday to install a security system. The broken windowpanes and mess inside proved the flimsy door-handle lock wouldn't keep anyone out, but she had to do something to combat her lack of control over her life, her own body and basically everything else in the world.

Head down, she trudged over to her green Mini Cooper, racking her brain for a reason why this was happening.

Why would someone be so desperate for her to sell? The house wasn't big. The land surrounding it wasn't particularly scenic or valuable and it was practically in the middle of nowhere, even by Nebraska standards. The Lakota Reservation was just up the road, but the only thing on this end was prairie. Tribal leaders announced last week that they were going to build the new casino on the eastern end of the reservation.

Unable to come up with a reasonable explanation, Beth slid behind the wheel. The car's engine purred to life and she steered it toward Dry Creek. She hadn't had any luck in her in-person search at the county clerk's office beyond finding a corporation name, but maybe she could find a clue to the buyer's identity in the online records.

Too late, she spotted the crater-sized pothole.

A tire dipped into the chasm. The car veered to the right.

Desperate to stay on the highway, she jerked the steering wheel left, overcorrecting and nearly shooting off the other side. As she pulled back into the correct lane, coffee sloshed out of the small opening on the top of her travel mug, soaking her hand and thigh.

She grabbed a gym towel from the passenger seat and looked back up.

A ten-point buck stood stock still in the middle of the two-lane road.

Anxiety rocketed through her body as she smashed the brake to the floor.

Nothing happened.

She pumped the pedal, each time slamming it to the floor in a vain attempt to stop the car's forward motion. Corn fields whizzed by as the car hurtled forward.

Panicking, she tried not to hyperventilate behind the wheel. Her choices were limited. Go head-to-head with the buck, which would decimate her tiny car and probably her in it, or swerve into the crops, hopefully avoiding the deep irrigation gullies often bordering the fields.

Icy dread froze her hands to the steering wheel. The seatbelt tightened against her chest. She fought to slow her breathing. In a heartbeat, she was an eight-year-old girl again, trapped upside down in her parents' station wagon, crying for a mother who could no longer hear her.

As her heart hammered, the Mini Cooper barreled toward the mesmerized deer.

She murmured a Hail Mary under her breath and pulled the wheel to the right.

Chapter Five

The airbag slammed into Beth's chest, sending her body backwards. Her head bounced against the headrest. Pain and panic exploded through her body.

Her throat clenched. The world darkened around the edges. She had to get out. Now.

Choking on the inflated airbag's chemical smell, she felt around for her seat belt clasp. God, what if she couldn't find it? Blood rushed through her ears. Sweat dripped down her forehead. She couldn't be trapped.

Not again.

Never again.

Her jittery fingers pushed against the clasp. It zipped across her body. Frantic, she slapped at the puffy airbag until it deflated enough to reach the door handle. She heaved the door open and stumbled out into the irrigation ditch.

Frigid water soaked through her jeans and spilled over the top of her cowboy boots.

She inhaled breath after breath of the cold October air that burned her nostrils, greedy and desperate, like a woman emerging from the depths of the ocean. Her heartbeat calmed. The world came back into focus.

Glancing back at her car, her stomach slid down to her wet toes.

Son of a bitch.

The front end had tipped forward into the gully, the hood folding up like an accordion. A foot of black water lapped at the mangled front end. The back tires rested on the bank nearest to the road.

Sucking on her bottom lip to keep it from quivering, she closed her eyes. *Just a car, Beth. It's a damn car. Besides it breaks down too often. You can handle this.*

When she opened her eyes again, the scene in front of her looked less like the end of the world and more like a manageable car crisis. Another manageable car crisis.

She stomped through the slushy ditch water and leaned inside the wreckage to swipe her gym bag from the floor in front of the passenger seat, then slogged her way up to the highway. The deer was nowhere to be found. Lucky him.

Grimacing, she punched in the number for her mechanic. Thanks to her many trips to Mad Mike's Mechanical, she'd memorized it months ago.

"Thanks for calling Mad Mike's. What can we do to make you happy?" Hailey's chipper voice carried over the phone's static connection.

"Hey, Hailey."

"Oh no, Beth. What's going on with that cute car of yours this time?"

"I lost at a game of chicken with a deer on Highway 28 and ended up in a ditch."

"Oh my goodness! Are you okay? Do you need an ambulance?"

"Thanks, but I'm okay." Shading her eyes against the early afternoon sun, she scanned the road for a landmark. "I'm near mile marker twelve. Can you send out the tow truck?"

"Sure thing, sweetie. Mike'll be right there."

After thirty minutes of alternating between swearing this time she'd get a new car and playing cellphone scrabble, the tow truck finally rumbled to a stop in front of her. Relief loosened the tightness in her shoulders and she stood, brushing dirt from the seat of her jeans.

The crunch of another set of tires on the gravel caught her attention and she glanced up to see a familiar dark blue pickup stop behind the tow truck. Her heart sped up and she smoothed her hair before she could stop herself.

Concern tightened Hank's square jaw when he stepped down from his truck and Beth's insides melted into warm goo. Damn that man.

Five days into a two-week vacation, he'd given up his Dry Creek County Sheriff uniform for jeans, a T-shirt and a scraggly beard that he somehow made appealing. Her fingers itched to feel the prickle of the three-day beard, to run through his thick brown hair that she knew from years of lustful observation curled if he let it grow to his collar. He was the stuff of dreams. Naughty, sweaty, tasty dreams.

The object of her desire strolled across the cracked asphalt to her side. The smell of fresh coffee wafted up from the paper cup in his large hands and mixed with the woodsy scent of his cologne.

"Are you okay?" Worry weighed heavy in his deep voice and he brushed a stray hair away from her face, his eyes searching for injuries.

Every objection to touching him evaporated and all her thoughts focused on how much she wanted to wrap her arms around his waist and soak up his strength.

"I do believe I can arrest you for looking at someone like that. You've got to be breaking some decency laws."

Taking a deep breath, she recovered her bearings. Mostly. "You're out of your jurisdiction, sheriff."

઒ૡૡ

Hank fisted his free hand and fought to calm his jumpy nerves. Yep, he was out of his jurisdiction, out of his league, out of luck and out of his mind for wanting Beth. Badly.

His gaze combed over her, from her silky brown hair to the tips of her red cowboy boots. Her glasses were a little cockeyed, but she didn't have a scratch on her and for the first time since he'd heard about the accident, something inside him loosened.

A cough interrupted his inspection. Hank and Beth turned toward the short, squat man in a red Mad Mike's Mechanical T-shirt kicking dirt with the tip of his steel-toed boot. Damn, he'd forgotten all about Mike and the reason they were both there. "You got her all hooked up?"

"Yep. Jus' need ya to move over a bit so I can get her pulled up from the ditch."

Before he could say a word, Beth strode to the other side of the road, her head high, purposefully not looking his way.

He shuffled over a few feet and watched as Mike pushed a button, setting off a cacophony of clanking chains. The chains pulled tight with a loud clang and that ridiculously small car Beth drove slid backwards up the ditch. It took Mike a few minutes to pull the car up, secure it to the trailer and begin the process of ensuring everything was safe for the drive back to his shop in Dry Creek.

Hank used the time to get a handle on the lust that had been riding roughshod over his body since he saw with his own eyes that Beth was okay. But he couldn't look away from Beth's curves framed by her V-neck black sweater and worn jeans. She stretched, extending one arm toward the clear blue sky and pushing her small tits forward. His cock transformed into steel and he unconsciously took a step forward.

Shit. He wanted her more than he'd ever wanted anyone, including Amanda when they first started dating.

It took him years to see through her manipulative ways and extricate himself from her razor-sharp talons. Not a good loser, Amanda swore he'd never find anyone as good as her, especially since he was just a washed-up ballplayer with a bum knee and a criminal justice degree. The thing was, she'd had him so twisted up during the final days of their marriage that he'd believed her. Some days he still did.

Maybe that's why Beth burned so hot yet acted so cold toward him, because she thought he wasn't worth her time.

"All righty then. You're all set." Mike slapped the Mini Cooper's bumper.

"Great." Beth lugged her gym bag up from the highway shoulder then crossed the road. "Can you drop me off at my house?"

Mike's gaze slid over to Hank as he wiped away the nonexistent sweat from his forehead with a greasy rag. "Um, well..."

"I'll give you a ride." Hank started toward his truck, chewing the inside of his cheek, nervous about how she'd react to the story he and Mike concocted. "Suzie threw up in Mike's cab and it smells like a sewer in there."

Oblivious to the defamation, the rotund feline slept curled in a ball on the cab's dashboard.

Mike kept his gaze locked on the pothole to the left of his back tire. "Yep. Wouldn't want you to have to spend time in there. Uh, that's why I brought Hank along."

Beth snorted, her suspicious gaze flickering between the men.

He didn't blame her; if Mike played poker as bad as he lied, there was no way Hank would have lost fifty dollars to him last night. Lucky for him, he'd been paying off that loss when the call came in about Beth's car.

"Front door service." Holding out his hands, palms up, he flashed the affable, baby-kissing grin he'd perfected during last fall's election. "Promise my truck does not smell like cat puke."

Sighing, Beth pivoted and walked to his truck. As she slid into the passenger seat, he nodded a silent thank you to Mike. Now he had the twenty-minute drive into Dry Creek to convince her to go out to dinner and a movie. Nothing life threatening. Really, how hard could it be?

As soon as he shut the driver's side door and the smell of her vanilla and lilac perfume teased his senses, his mind went blank.

"Why is Mike giving you a thumbs up?"

Glancing at the rearview mirror as he pulled away from the tow truck, he spotted Mike standing in the middle of the highway with a smartass grin on his face and his thumb stuck up as if he were hitching a ride. Mike always was subtle. "Who knows why he does half the things he does."

Beth settled back into the seat and proceeded to stare out the window, ignoring him completely. A million idiotic conversation starters rattled around his head, but he couldn't get his dry mouth to form the words. The silence ate away at Hank's nerves. Glancing out of the corner of his eye, he checked her out. The woman sat straight as a board, nervous energy pulsing from her brown skin, finding its outlet as she fiddled with the green nylon strap of her gym bag.

He should say something. Anything. He was a grown man driving with a woman he'd known for most of his life. When had it gotten so hard to talk to her?

The sugar beet factory loomed on the horizon, with the big box stores only a little bit farther on. In another few minutes they'd be in Dry Creek proper. A couple of stoplights later and they'd be in front of her adobe bungalow on Kaftan Street. His heartbeat sped up like a thirteen-year-old nerd's walking up to the prettiest, most popular girl in school.

A block from her house, he couldn't take the silence anymore and blurted out the first thing that came to mind. "So, I heard Sarah Jane made a mint when she sold her place. You thinking of selling your grandparents' place?"

Beth spun around in her seat and nailed him with a deadly glare. "I'm never selling, and if you know who the asshole is who's trying to intimidate me into selling, you can tell him that it won't work."

Someone threatened her? Anger squeezed his chest. He slammed on the brakes in front of her house, making his truck tires squeal. "What the hell are you talking about? And why is this the first I'm hearing about it?"

She stopped fidgeting with the bag's strap. Her whole body went still as her big brown eyes regarded him. Uncertainty flashed across her face and her forehead crinkled. Her gaze flicked away for an instant. When she looked at him again with a stubborn tilt to her chin, his temple throbbed.

He wasn't going to like this, not one bit. Stubborn woman was going to make him certifiably nuts.

"Never mind, I'm sure it's nothing." She waved her long fingers in the air as if brushing off an invisible inconvenience. "Thanks for the ride home."

He grabbed her left hand as her right reached for the door handle. Her warmth shocked his fingers and slithered up his arm. "Bullshit. I've known you since you were young enough to eat your own boogers. You wouldn't have said it if it was nothing."

Yanking ineffectively to free her hand, she shot him a dirty look. "Let me go, Hank. It's none of your damn business."

Pulling her close so that their faces nearly touched, he fought to rein in the caveman urge to drag her somewhere safe and hide her away from anything bad in the world. "If it involves you, it *is* my business."

Damn straight. As soon as he dropped her off, he'd do some snooping of his own. He knew a few deputies in neighboring Council County who didn't appreciate Sheriff Wilcox's brand of flexible ethics.

Time to call in some favors, find out what the hell was going on and fix it.

Her eyes went wide, showing off the gold flecks in her dark irises. She inhaled a shaky breath. "Look," she whispered. "I know you're Claire's big brother and we've known each other forever, but I can't let you involve yourself in this. It's not in your jurisdiction. It's not your house. You're like a brother to me and I don't want you to get sucked into my trouble."

A dark laugh rumbled up from some aching part of his soul. "Like a brother." The words would have hurt like a kick to the balls if she hadn't been lying through her teeth. "You're full of it, Beth. I know it and you know it. The way your body reacts to mine is far from sisterly. You want me just as damn bad as I want you. What I can't figure out is why you're denying it."

With a ferocious tug, she pulled her captured hand free. "What you're feeling is your business, but I want you the hell out of mine."

She thrust the door open, hooked her gym bag over one shoulder and hopped down from the truck.

He wished it was that easy. Something happened to him during dinner at Juanita's and cemented at Claire's house as soon as his hand settled onto her hip and he pulled her closer in the hallway's dim light. In that half second of hesitation before she relaxed in his arms, he'd never been so afraid in all his life. But as soon as he'd tasted her lips, all of that faded to the background.

Time for a play fake. "I'll leave you alone on one condition."

Eyeing him warily, she crossed her arms. "What's that?"

Hank got out of the truck and strolled over to the passenger side, stopping next to her. At five feet, nine inches, she would fit perfectly against his taller frame. He had to stop himself from reaching out and pulling her to him. "Kiss me."

Her mouth gaped open and she slammed the passenger door shut before marching up the short paved path to her porch, her sweet ass swinging the whole time.

Lust slammed into him, hardening his cock and threatening the zipper on his jeans.

She never said no to a dare.

"If you still only think of me in brotherly terms, I won't bother you again. Unless, of course, you're chicken."

She stopped with her back to him. "One kiss?"

"One little kiss."

A fall breeze brushed the tips of her brown hair across her back and she straightened her shoulders. Spinning around, she made her way back to him with a fuck-you strut. Stopping just short of his feet, she dropped her gym bag. It hit the pavement with a thud, the whole world seeming to have gone silent around them.

"Let's get it over with."

Something primal inside of him howled its approval. He wanted to devour her full lips then and there.

Stick to the plan, dude.

He held firm. Barely. "Okay, you can kiss me."

"Wait a minute—"

"You're the one who says there's nothing between us, so I figure you should set the tone of the kiss. It's up to you to disprove my theory."

"Of all the stupid things." She huffed out a breath. "Fine."

Hank held his breath, hoping all his bluster would pay off. God, this woman undid him.

She laid her soft hand against his chest. There was no way she could miss the hammering behind his ribs. Navy-blue nails shone bright against the red of his cotton shirt. Her shoulders twitched with a shiver. A flicker of doubt shook him. Maybe she'd ignored him after the party for a reason.

Then her lips touched his. Chocolate and caramel coffee teased his taste buds as their tongues twisted around each other. Lightning shot through his system, turning his muscles to steel. He clenched his hands to keep from filling them with her high, round ass and grinding her against his hard cock.

With a low moan, she pressed her body into his, rubbing her perfect, handful-sized tits across his chest. Her fingers curved around his head, tangled in his hair and severed the tenuous hold he had on his self-control. Like a starving man presented with a buffet, he feasted on the kiss. His hands roamed to the bottom of her soft wool sweater, snuck underneath the hem and caressed the soft skin above the low waist of her jeans.

Her vanilla perfume surrounded him as he lowered his mouth to taste the sweetness of her neck. He lost himself to the hungry lust streaming through his veins and the moaning woman in his arms. There was no street, no gawking neighbors, no one else in the world.

"Hank, stop." Beth's breath brushed against his cheek.

More plea than demand, her words sliced through his euphoria. Unwilling to let her go yet, he lifted his head but kept his fingers tucked into her waistband. Still tasting her on his lips, he couldn't form any words.

A flush pinked her cheeks as she pursed her kiss-swollen lips. "So...that's...out of the way."

Her hand shook when she patted him on the chest, her fingers lingering for a few seconds over his pounding heart. With a sigh, she pulled out of his embrace and trudged up to the house, never looking back.

She thought this was over? After a kiss like that? His balls couldn't be any bluer if they were made of blueberries. For a smart woman, she sure wasn't thinking straight.

"Like hell," he growled.

Chapter Six

The cinnamon roll's gooey, sugary goodness melted on Beth's tongue and she closed her eyes to better savor the ecstasy. If this couldn't make a Monday better, she couldn't imagine what would. Margret Goodwin may be the biggest gossip in Dry Creek, but her divine baking ability made a visit to her shop a must.

"So where'd you disappear to during the party?" Claire asked.

Beth spotted the poof of Margret's frizzy platinum hair sticking up over the top of the half-full lemonade dispenser. Making eye contact with Claire, Beth shrugged a shoulder toward the counter at Margret's inept attempt at covert eavesdropping. The bell above the bakery's door jangled and Margret scurried away from her hiding spot to help the newcomer.

Humor sparkled in Claire's brown eyes. She swiped the last bite of cinnamon roll from their shared plate and stuffed it into her mouth.

Playacting a pout, Beth stuck out her tongue.

"Ha. I grew up with three brothers, you never had a chance," Claire said with a grin.

"True, but that means the icing is all mine."

The fight for the last bit of a shared treat was a tradition dating back to second grade, when Beth introduced Claire to the honey-covered, fried pastry decadence known as a sopapilla. Sure, this time Claire had gotten the last of the cinnamon roll, but the frosting was a worthy consolation prize. Scooping the creamy, white goodness onto a finger and into her mouth, Beth savored its sweetness. It would all go straight to her well-padded ass, but it was worth it. Her eyes closed, she barely noticed when the air shifted around her.

"Now, where have I seen that look on your face before?" Hank plopped down into one of the pink-and-white-striped chairs at the table. He greeted Claire with a quick, "Hey, sis."

The azure shade of his button-up shirt brought out the green hues in his hazel eyes, drawing her in and promising a future of warm spring days and everything perfect and good. With Hank's gaze locked on her, mesmerizing her, she barely heard his chair scrape against the floor as he scooted it closer until their knees touched.

Beth froze, her finger still in her mouth, her skin vibrating until electricity spread up her tense thigh to her fast dampening panties. Shit. How did he do this to her through so many layers of clothes? Imagine her response if they were naked. Her skin flushed. *Better yet, don't think of that.*

"Can I borrow your spoon?" His words were innocent but the gravelly tone promised all sorts of indecent experiences.

Her nipples jutted against her lacy bra and she thanked God the padding hid proof of her desire.

Steam floated up from his paper coffee cup and he dumped three packets of sugar into the dark brew. Grabbing the spoon, he wriggled his eyebrows at her.

With all the grace of a bull in a china shop, Margret delivered a chocolate sprinkle donut to the table and ever so slowly walked to the nearby counter, where she rearranged the cups, peeking over her shoulder every few moments.

Claire crossed her arms, her head cocked to one side as she stared at her oldest brother. "Sure, we'd love to have you join us, Hank. Thanks for asking."

"Don't mind if I do, thanks, sis." His gaze never left Beth. "But I can only stay for a minute. I wanted to make sure there haven't been any more calls about your grandparents' place."

She couldn't let him get involved. Look at how she reacted to him in public. In private, she'd never keep her panties on. That couldn't happen. Another jingle at the door saved her from having to answer.

One of Hank's deputies poked his head in the door. "Ready to go?"

"In a minute, Keith." Hank made no move to get up. "So, any new incidents?"

"Nope." Sunday had been uneventful. No more damage or threats was good, but she wished she had learned something in her online records search. Everything she'd found revealed only a tangle of information about a vague corporation with a ghost for a CEO.

"Good. I've made a few inquiries—"

"What do you mean? I told you to stay out of it."

"Darlin', you know that's not going to happen. How's the car?"

The abrupt topic switch threw her off track. "Mike's checking it out now, said he'd have an estimate for me in a few days."

"Well, you know I'm happy to give you a ride anytime." His hand dropped to her leg, right above the knee and his thumb rubbed against her sensitive inner thigh.

Unable to form a thought, she mumbled incoherently.

Nodding, he scooted his chair back and stood before giving her a quick peck on the cheek.

Electricity jolted across her skin at the scratch of his vacation beard against her jaw. A shiver of desire ran down her spine when he pulled away.

"See ya soon, darlin'."

Reflexively, her hand went to her cheek and rubbed as she watched him strut out of the bakery.

"Oh my God," Margret muttered from beside the cash register. "Wait until I tell Susan." The baker uttered a tiny squeal and made a beeline to the back office.

Great. By the time the gossip got around town, the story will be that she and Hank had gotten down and dirty in the middle of the bakery while using phallic-shaped donuts as sex toys. Gotta love living in a small town.

"What in the hell just happened?" Claire sounded as if she'd had the wind knocked out of her.

Beth knew the feeling. "I have no idea."

"Boloney sausage."

As always, Claire's prettied-up version of bullshit made her laugh. "He's your brother. Totally off limits. Anyway, my life's crazy enough lately without adding in your fucks-everything-that-moves brother."

"Hey now, that's my brother you're talking about."

"Yep, and I believe you were the one who called him that just a few weeks ago."

"No, I said dates-everything-that-moves brother. You're the one whose dirty mind took it down that path." Her warm hand covered Beth's suddenly cold one. "But what makes him off limits? Don't give me crap about him sleeping around, you and I both know small-town gossip blows everything out of proportion. He's a great guy. You're awesome. Really, you two would be perfect for each other."

Beth slid her fingers from her friend's grasp and brushed the crumbs on the table into a pile.

Claire had never been without a loving family. She didn't understand how awful it was to lose it. She hadn't grown up without parents, hadn't found her grandfather dead on the laundry room floor or watched dementia push her grandmother deeper and deeper into her sepia-toned memories. Beth had become a woman knowing good things come to an end way too soon and that the people you loved always left.

Even those who hadn't arrived yet.

Beth fiddled with her spoon as guilt rose up. Best friends didn't keep secrets from each other, but she hadn't told Claire about the hysterectomy. Talking about it would make it real, solidify it as fact, and she wasn't ready for that yet.

Claire cleared her throat. "Earth to Beth."

"Sorry, I've got a lot going on right now."

"So what's making you nuts?"

Beth hadn't wanted to burden her best friend with her troubles. However, judging from the spill-it-now wrinkle on Claire's brow, the time had come.

After looking around to make sure Margaret was still ensconced somewhere relaying gossip about Hank's kiss, she leaned forward, her elbows resting on the table's cold Formica top. "So, you know how everyone near my grandparents' house has been selling to some mystery buyer?"

Bringing her up to speed about the late-night threats delivered over the phone by a heavy-breathing man, the nasty texts, the vandalism, Sheriff Wilcox's response and her answer to his recommendation that she sell took ten minutes, punctuated by Claire's gasps.

"Oh man, I bet the sheriff's head almost popped off his body when you told him what he could do with his advice to sell." She broke off a piece of Hank's abandoned chocolate sprinkle donut and popped it in her mouth.

"Yep, you could say that. He slammed the door shut so hard the windows rattled."

"That man's always been an ass. Hank says the other sheriffs avoid him like the plague." Her friend's brown eyes narrowed. "So why haven't you told me or Hank about this sooner?"

"Up until this week, it didn't seem that serious. Just some angry phone calls and such. Hell, most of the people who live out near my grandparents' house hate my guts right now for not selling. Sara Jane told me the other day that if I don't sell, the developer is threatening to renege on his promise to buy everyone else's land." She paused for a breath. "Besides, you and Jake are finally drama-free after that psycho Burlington went to jail. I didn't want to wreck that."

"You are such a dork," Claire chided. "We've been best friends since grade school. What matters to you, matters to me. Now, I know you—what have you done to figure out who's behind all this?"

The bell above the bakery door chimed and Beth jumped in her seat. One of the construction workers tearing down the burnt remains of The Harvest Bistro across the street strolled in. This whole situation had her on edge more than she wanted to admit.

At least her quick trip to Vegas would provide a distraction. Giving her first presentation at the National Estate Attorneys Conference would take all her concentration and give her some distance from angry neighbors and pushy developers.

"I've looked through as many of the public records as I could get ahold of. Every time I find a company name, it turns out to be a front." Beth sipped her warm brew. It slid down her throat, heating her body from the inside out. "The whole thing stinks to high heaven and that fool Wilcox is in it up to his third chin."

"You really need to tell Hank about all this."

"My grandparents' house is in Council County. Hank's jurisdiction ends at the Dry Creek County line."

"Uh-huh, so what's with him branding you like a prized calf, because you and I both know that's what that kiss was all about."

Her heart raced at the idea and she clasped her hands tighter around her mug to keep them from shaking. "Nothing."

"Has he asked you out?"

Heat flared in Beth's cheeks.

Eyes wide with curiosity, Claire leaned in. "Oh my God, did you sleep with him?"

"No!" She straightened in her chair, putting as much distance as possible between her and her best friend. The words tumbled out anyway. "We kissed. That's all. It didn't mean a thing."

Claire shook her head, sending her auburn hair waving around her shoulders. "Yep, keep telling yourself that, Beth."

The alarm on her cellphone vibrated and she swiped it off the tabletop. "Come on, we gotta head out to the airport. Thanks again for dropping me off."

"Hey, what are friends for?" Claire grabbed her plate and Beth's empty coffee cup and placed them on the counter before they walked out the door. "You know, Hank's leaving tomorrow for a boys' poker trip to Vegas. Chris and Sam are already out there. God, I can't imagine what trouble my three brothers are going to cook up." She grinned at Beth. "Maybe you'll run into him. It would be the perfect opportunity to ask for help in a neutral environment, and you know, if things happen to get all hot and heavy..."

Beth yanked open the car door and slid into the passenger seat. "That is not going to happen." She snapped her seat belt closed.

Claire plopped down into the driver's seat. "Mmm-hmmm. We'll see."

"Don't even think about it."

Pure deviousness crinkled the corner of Claire's brown eyes. "I have no idea what you're talking about." She turned on the radio and started singing along to an old Motown song in an off-key voice that should only be heard in the shower.

Giggling, Beth joined in, her own voice as jarringly out of tune as her friend's. Somewhere in

Dry Creek, the dogs had to be howling along with them.

After a short car ride to the regional airport, a quick check-in at the kiosk and an uncomfortable groping from the security agent, Beth climbed the stairs of the small commercial jet.

Walking down the narrow walkway between the seats, she kept her gaze glued to the seat numbers for twelve-A. There it was, two rows up, a window seat. Things were looking up.

The woman in front of her stowed a carry-on bag in the overhead storage, then sat down, giving Beth a view of the coach passengers buckling in. Her stomach did a triple flip.

Hank looked up at her from twelve-B. "You wouldn't be stalking me now, would you? Because I probably wouldn't mind."

Chapter Seven

*T*he fates were against her.

Beth's black skirt suddenly felt two sizes too small as heat spread through her limbs. Her stomach sank and fluttered at the same time and she double-checked her seat assignment. Twelve-A. Damn.

"You sitting down or what, lady?" The short guy in a business suit behind her not-so-gently nudged her with his oversized carry on, hitting her square in the ass. She flashed him a dirty look and took in the size of his suitcase. The zipper looked about to pop. There was no way in hell that thing would fit in the overhead compartment.

"Hold your horses, I'm moving." But her feet, encased in pointed-toed black heels, refused to go forward.

The line got restless behind her and the grumbling increased. Only a handful of empty seats remained in coach. Judging by the number of grumpy people still in line, switching seats wasn't going to be an option. Time to put on her big-girl panties and suck it up. The flight was only two hours. She could handle that. Right?

She pushed her glasses back up the bridge of her nose. "I don't know how you managed to make this happen."

"Just luck, I guess." Amusement flashed across Hank's face and he sat up straight in the aisle seat. "Do you need me to get out or can you squeeze by?"

Beth steeled herself. "I can get by."

There was just enough space for her to shuffle through, but not by much. Her bare calves brushed his knees and she faltered for a moment, grabbing the headrest of the seat in front.

Grasping her hips, he steadied her. Each of his long fingers burned an imprint through her skirt and onto her sensitive skin. Body on high alert and anticipating pleasure, she shivered under his touch. His fingers tightened, his thumbs pressing into the tender top curve of her ass. A strangled sound, half groan and half sigh, escaped her lips.

Like a siren blaring in the far-off distance, the audible proof of her arousal brought her back to reality. Embarrassed he could do this to her so easily and in the middle of a packed airplane, she ignored her instinct to lower herself onto his lap.

"Steady there." Hank's voice had gone husky. His fingers flexed over the thin material of her skirt.

"I'm fine. Thank you." The words came out in a shaky whisper.

Holding her breath, she sidestepped the last few inches to her seat. As soon as her legs cleared his, a chill covered her calves from the loss of his body heat. Sitting, she stuffed her leather briefcase under the seat in front of her. The flashes of excitement skittering along her skin told her he watched her every move.

Studiously looking out the window at the airport employees bustling around on the tarmac, she reached for her seat belt, her fingers accidentally brushing his thigh. Biting her bottom lip to keep from making any more tell-tale noises, she pulled the belt across her lap and snapped it closed. After tightening it until it was snug against her waist, she watched the baggage handlers tossing suitcases into the belly of the plane. Her purple suitcase flew into the baggage compartment. Well, at least she'd packed all of her breakable items in her briefcase.

"Still bothers you, huh?" His voice slid across her skin like a warm breeze as he leaned closer to peer out the window.

"It's okay, there're only clothes in it."

"Not your suitcase, this." His warm hands covered hers, stilling them.

Unknowingly, she'd been tugging at the seat belt, some part of her needing to double-check it would hold. The car accident must've shook her up more than she'd realized. Despite everything, his concern touched her. It had been twenty years since her parents' fatal car crash. She'd been trapped for hours, hanging upside down, secured to her seat by her seatbelt. It had saved her life.

"I'm okay."

He gave her hands a light squeeze. "Good."

The captain's announcement about expected weather conditions during the flight stopped any further exchange. Hank settled back into his seat and the little plane picked up speed, bouncing a bit as it barreled down the runway.

Blood pounded in her ears and her tongue stuck to the roof of her mouth as that old familiar fear plucked her nerves. Man, she hated flying. Clutching the armrest in a white-knuckle grip, she forced herself to breathe in slowly, hold it a second and then exhale. Her stomach dropped as the plane left the ground and she squeezed her eyes shut. All Beth could picture was her mom's long brown hair spread wide across the ceiling of the station wagon, her mouth hanging open and the wet sound of her gasps echoing in the silent night.

"You know I've been fantasizing about you since I was twenty-two?" Hank's hand covered her smaller one. "I came home after boot camp and bam; my little sister's best friend had turned into a stone-cold fox."

His words pulled her away from the terror of that night. Grateful, she squeezed his hand.

Lowering his lips until they nearly touched her ear, he hushed his voice to a throaty whisper. "I've spent a lot of time alone, thinking of how that ass of yours would feel in my hands. Hard or soft? How much would it bounce if I gave it a little slap?"

Her gaze jumped around the plane as a fierce blush burned her cheeks. Had anyone heard? "Shut up, people will hear you." She glanced back and spotted two junior attorneys from her office three rows behind them.

"So?"

"So?" The single word came out louder than she'd intended, drawing the attention of the passengers across the aisle, exactly what she'd been trying to avoid. Smiling weakly at their irritated faces, she quieted her voice. "I do not want everyone to think that I'm the latest in your parade of women."

He shrugged his wide shoulders. "Sure, I've dated a few women since the divorce, but I don't think you can call it a parade."

A few? A few? If he called twenty-eight a few, then he needed to rethink his math abilities. "Do you want me to name them all?"

"So you've been keeping track, eh?" He sat up straighter in his chair, pride beaming from his hazel eyes.

Damn. He picked up on that. Flustered, Beth wished she could think of something to say to wipe that smug smile off his face but whatever brain synapses controlled her smartass comeback function failed. Her mind stayed stubbornly blank.

The light green flecks in his eyes disappeared as the irises darkened. "I've been chasing after you for weeks now."

She fiddled with her skirt hem, not daring to make eye contact or he'd know how much staying away from him cost her.

"Sure, I've dated other women, but they're not you—and I want you."

His words slapped her across the face.

Don't cry. Whatever you do, don't cry.

Biting her lip, she said nothing.

"After Claire's party, I thought we'd turned a corner. But you're even more skittish around me than before. So, what's going to happen, Beth?"

A thunk reverberated under her seat as the pilot raised the plane's wheels. She'd give anything to be able to say yes to him even just once, but she'd already lost too many people to do that again. "Nothing is going to happen between us."

The vein in his temple pulsated and his mouth formed a grim line. "Okay, I guess I have my answer." He leaned back in his seat and closed his eyes. "But I'm not going to stop asking."

By the time the fasten-your-seat-belt light blinked off a few minutes later, Hank's breathing was slow and steady.

Her thoughts in a jumble, she reached for her briefcase. She needed work to distract her from the lusty heat building in her belly, and lower. Work always took her total concentration.

She grabbed the folder labeled Haverstan Limited. The company name was all she'd been able to find in the real estate records filed after Mrs. Hunihan and the rest of her neighbors had agreed to sell. The deal was set to close in another week, but only if she agreed to sell too. Flipping through the sheaf of papers inside, she grabbed one at random. The Nebraska Secretary of State's Office logo, an identifiable if not overly creative outline of the state, stretched across the top of the page. According to the state, Haverstan's CEO was one Robert Reynolds of Stickland, Nebraska.

The problem? Robert Reynolds was dead and had been for about ten years.

A reporter with the local weekly newspaper in Stickland had e-mailed her a copy of Reynolds' obit. He'd lived a good life, raised corn and a trio of daughters until he'd dropped dead of a massive heart attack at the age of sixty-six while shopping for a new combine at John Deere.

The estate attorney in her wondered if he'd gotten everything squared away before he'd died. Many farmers didn't, they expected to work their land until they hit ninety. Most were wrong.

Checking out the sleeping Hank from the corner of her eye, she wondered if she could get him to do a DMV search for Robert Reynolds to see if another lived in Stickland. Only two thousand three hundred and forty-one people lived in the tiny farming community as of the last census, meaning the chances of two unrelated Robert Reynoldses living in the same small town were pretty slim.

Hank shifted in his seat and laid his head down on her shoulder. She bobbed her arm, trying to dislodge him, but he didn't budge.

"Stop moving." He smacked his lips together. "I promise not to drool." Snuggling in, he never opened his eyes.

His weight pressed against her, solid and unyielding. Claustrophobia should have set in, the fear of being trapped clawing at her. Instead, his body warmed her and calmed her nerves. It felt good. Too good. Shit, she couldn't even scoot by him in the plane without getting hot and bothered. If she enlisted his help in this mess, she'd be another notch on his bedpost within a week. Then she'd have to stop avoiding her childless future and face it head on.

Not yet. Beth chose to put the pain into a little box and shut it away. Someday, maybe.

Tossing the page onto the file folder spread open on the tray table, she harrumphed in frustration. Using her unhampered left arm, she pulled another page free of the file.

Her heart stopped.

A yellow note covered in unfamiliar handwriting was stuck to the corner of the paper.

I'm begging you. Sell. It's gone too far to stop. There's no other way. Please, before it's too late!

The cramped words were scrawled across the two-inch-by-two-inch note, written in blue ink with an unfamiliar heavy hand that had broken through the bright paper on the exclamation point's dot. Peeling it from right to left, she eased the note away from the larger page. Her hand shook as she held it up. Heart hammering, she tried to push down her growing panic.

Who?

When?

How?

She didn't have a single answer.

That was it. She needed Hank's help. She didn't have a choice.

But she did have a little time. Three days to be exact; the length of the conference. As soon as she was back home, she'd ask for Hank's help. Even if it was out of his jurisdiction, he'd know what to do.

Decision made, her breathing mellowed. After all, nothing was going to happen to her while she was in Vegas.

Chapter Eight

*S*uccess was only a dead girl away.

A woman, really, but to Sarah Jane Hunihan, they were all just girls yet to be turned into cynical bitches by fate's cruel sense of humor.

Alone in a bathroom at Las Vegas' Paris Casino, Sarah Jane allowed herself a moment to let her well-maintained facade slip. Sliding down the gold cap of her mauve lipstick until it clicked, she smacked her lips together with a little pop. Glancing at the ornate, gilded bathroom mirror, Sarah Jane adjusted the upturned flip at the end of her steel-gray bob.

She'd had the cut forever and refused to give it up. Every time she looked in the mirror it was a reminder of her former self. Her weak self.

Let the world think she was a silly old woman obsessed with stamping, scrapbooks and church bake sales, it made getting away with things so much easier. For twenty-two years, she'd craved revenge. When the Lakota announced they were building a reservation casino, her plans for retribution fell into place.

Straightening her spine, just starting to develop a curve, she strode to the bathroom door. Decades ago, she'd transformed herself from that simpering secretary Ed Webster ruined.

Still, she held on to the pain and humiliation all these years later. The bitter emotions twisted together to destroy the numbness that had sunk into her very bones when she'd realized she'd meant nothing to him. She never had.

He'd never planned to leave his wife as he'd promised. All she had to do was give up their secret baby, he'd whispered. And she'd done it, learning too late what a lying bastard he was. Some other woman had swaddled their son. Counted his toes. Breathed in the baby-powder scent of his soft skin.

It had taken years to find her son. But she'd done it. And what did his bastard father do? He'd made noises the boy wasn't his, but Sarah Jane knew better.

Ed had ignored and denied his own son in favor of Beth Martinez.

Beth had come to work at the Webster and Carter Estate Firm, her office a few doors down from Sarah Jane's. She'd turned into Ed Webster's favorite. Not their son, who he refused to acknowledge. No. He showered his attention on that little bitch.

Now Beth was the only obstacle standing in the way of complete revenge. That changed tonight. She'd leveraged the plentiful results of twenty years of pinching pennies on the land deal that would destroy Ed. No one, especially not Beth Martinez, would take it away from her.

Sarah Jane's arthritic fingers protested when she wrapped them around the doorknob. If only the pain medication wasn't so expensive, she'd take it every day, but she sacrificed for the greater payoff. Tomorrow the little yellow pill and her successful removal of Beth would ease away the pain.

Grinning, she joined the throngs of people strolling down the fake cobblestone street at the

Paris Casino. She took in the sky-painted ceiling, forever daylight, with its puffy white clouds and the smell of freshly made crepes from the shops. A tarted-up woman in sky-high spiked heels bobbled across the uneven floor. Dumb girl.

Sarah Jane had been like her once. Not anymore. Her orthopedic shoes kept her feet planted firmly on the ground.

Her phone jingled above the piped-in French music of the casino. "Hello?'

"Something's going to go wrong." The worry in his voice carried over the music.

"Well, hello to you too, my sweet son." Again? How many times could she have the same conversation with him? "You worry too much, darling."

His foster mothers must have coddled him constantly for him to have grown up to be so whiney. Yet more fault to lay at his father's feet. If only she'd tracked her son down sooner.

"But, she's not going to get hurt. Right?" The tension in his voice spilled through the phone line.

"Of course not. We're just going to scare her a bit." Pausing for effect, she sat on an upholstered bench inside a store selling gaudy, overpriced shoes. "It is *we*, isn't it? You haven't decided to abandon your mother now that we've finally found each other? I don't think I could survive that."

"You know I wouldn't do that to you." The words rushed out of his mouth, concern tightening his tone.

"You told me all about being stuck in foster families who didn't understand you or love you like real ones would. I've tried to create a home for you. A real home. The kind of safe, loving home you missed out on when you were shuffled from family to family, but I'm just not feeling like we've developed a true mother-son bond."

"What have I done?"

Picking up a ridiculous Lucite stiletto heel, she wondered who would wear such a tasteless item. "I don't know; you seem so distant right now. I was devastated when your father forced me to give you up and then deserted me. When I found out your adoptive parents abandoned you to foster care, it nearly killed me. I'm sure I can't live through that again. If you left me now, why, I don't know what I'd do."

"I'm not like him. I love you."

She replaced the shoe before the saleswoman could try to corner her. "Do you?"

"Yes."

"Then stop fighting me on this." She couldn't keep the snap from her voice. "You know it's for the best."

"But she's not going to get hurt?"

"Hurt? No, I would never harm another human being. You're breaking my heart for even thinking that." Sarah Jane kept her mouth shut and stared at her nails while she counted. *One Mississippi. Two Mississippi. Three Mississippi.* She wouldn't get to fifteen before he broke. *Four Mississippi. Five Mississippi. Six Mississippi.*

"I'm sorry, mother. I am."

Smothering her smile, she forced a tremble into her voice. "So you trust me?"

"A hundred percent."

Hearing the submission in his voice, she strolled out of the store and toward the casino's front door.

"Then know everything will go as planned. I have to go now, darling. It's time for dinner."

She clicked the phone shut and dropped it into her purse before he had a chance to say goodbye. What a namby-pamby man he'd become. Things would have been different if she'd raised him. She'd have done it right. Once her plan came to fruition, she'd make up for that lapse.

When Sarah Jane had discovered Beth would be in Las Vegas for a national conference, the solution came to her immediately. A small-town girl gets taken down by big-city violence. It couldn't be any more perfect if Beth had planned her own death. She'd whispered the right words into the right ear at the law office and here she was, ready to put the final part of her plan into motion.

Stepping off the cobblestones onto the bright carpet of the casino, she tried to ignore the tackiness around her. God, she loathed Vegas. The bright lights and gaping tourists everywhere. Street people shoving escort advertisements into your hand as soon as you stepped outside your hotel.

She swallowed her distaste for this tacky cesspool because she deserved the money. No. She deserved her revenge. He owed her and it was time to pay. Two decades was a long time to wait for justice. And the look on his face when he realized what she'd done? That she'd caused his ultimate downfall? Priceless.

Sarah Jane dipped her hand inside the small side pocket of her gold brocade jacket and caressed the paper envelope, so small it could only hold the GHB. It had been so easy to steal it from Julie Hallerson's medicine cabinet during a scrapbooking meeting. Julie wouldn't miss a little of it, she'd had plenty of the prescription on hand to treat her fibromyalgia. Best of all, no one would be able to tie Sarah Jane to the drug if the plan went awry.

The hotel doors whooshed open in front of her and a blast of hot air landed heavy on her face. The valet opened the door of the waiting yellow taxi.

"Where to?" The driver's beady dark eyes watched her in the rearview mirror.

Time to get into character. She let her spine slouch to accentuate the curve in her upper back. Exhaling, she raised her eyebrows and curled her lips into an open, grandmotherly smile. The driver relaxed and smiled condescendingly.

"The Orion, please. My friend is having a celebratory dinner."

And soon she'd be celebrating as well.

Chapter Nine

An hour after the company-sponsored dinner, Beth sat stone still on a couch inside Club Reaction, the world swerving around her in a blurry haze. Across the low bar table, Sandy, the estate attorney from Ohio, zoomed in and out of focus as she droned on about her latest case to a rapt audience.

The conversation filtered into her brain like a legal jargon game of Mad Libs. She clanked down her champagne flute on the small table in front of her harder than she'd intended.

A scantily clad buxom server appeared immediately at her side. "Would you like another glass?"

Beth's stomach turned a few times. "No thanks. One's my limit."

That must have been some champagne to have affected her so strongly. Closing her eyes to block out the scene spinning in front of her, she focused all her mental energy on taking slow and steady breaths. Relaxing back into the cushions, she let the sensual pleasure of the velvet against her bare legs spread throughout her body until she felt as if she could melt right into the couch. Really, would it be so bad to just let go like that?

A man's booming laugh—one she knew as well as her own—rang out over the crowd's noise and made her body vibrate with want. Her skin sizzled with anticipation. Like a woman in a dream, she accepted the inevitability of making that man hers.

She eased her eyes open and searched for the source of the laughter on the club's crowded dance floor. From her vantage point in the private seating area above the main bar, she scanned the fuzzy crush of barely clothed women and their muscle-bound, perfectly coiffed dates. A sea of faces moved in time with the music's staccato beat, but the laughing man wasn't among them.

Her palpable disappointment at not being able to find him confused her, scaring her into a moment of clarity. Something was seriously wrong. She'd had so much fun talking at dinner, she hadn't eaten much. Maybe the mixture of low blood sugar and a glass of champagne had submarined her.

Digging her short, unpolished fingernails into the palms of her hands, she fought for control. A sudden clammy sweat dampened the nape of her neck as she sought out a focal point to center herself. She picked Sandy's bright red lipstick, which stood out even in the club's dim light. With her gaze locked onto Sandy's mouth, everything stopped spinning and a heavy lethargy descended. Her eyelids drooped.

A tiny scream of panic echoed in Beth's head. She couldn't pass out in front of her colleagues.

She had to get out of here, go back to her room a few hotels down the Las Vegas strip and sleep it off before she humiliated herself in public.

This is why she hardly drank. She hated the out-of-control fuzziness of it all. But she'd only had one glass of champagne to celebrate the success of her lecture during the National Estate Attorneys

Association's annual conference. Still, she felt as if she'd gulped down the whole bottle of bubbly like a sorority girl with a bottle of peach schnapps during pledge week.

She pushed herself upward into a standing position, fighting the inertia swamping her limbs. A wave of dizziness overwhelmed her. Beth threw her arms out in an attempt to counteract her wobbling knees and weaving upper body.

The unavoidability of her fall penetrated her hazy mind, spiking her heart rate.

She tilted toward the table littered with empty martini glasses, and before momentum swung her onto her face, a strong arm wrapped around her waist.

Relief noodled her limbs and she sagged into the solid chest behind her. A familiar woodsy scent teased her senses. A quick visual sweep of the area revealed everyone's attention remained focused on Sandy, her low-cut dress and her tale of estate-planning woe.

"Thhhhh-ank you." Beth's thick tongue slurred out the words.

"No problem." Her white knight turned her around. "Let's get you back to your room, lightweight."

Her heart skipped. Just when she thought she'd been saved from disgrace, fate laughed in her face and heaped mortification upon her.

Hank. Of course, he had to have been her rescuer.

Cheeks flushed with embarrassment, she tried to wriggle free. His heat seeped through the thin material of her navy-blue wrap dress. Although it was closed tight, allowing only a sliver of skin to show, Beth felt exposed and vulnerable. As she looked up into his hazel eyes, the world stopping turning. Deep worry lines carved crevices into his forehead.

"Not a good idea unless you want to fall flat on your face." He pulled her tighter against his hard body.

Unable to stop herself, she brushed a thumb across his warm brow, and the wrinkles smoothed beneath her caress. A thrill skittered down her spine. Why did she always fight the attraction? Damned if she could remember. She wiggled closer to him, brushing against the growing bulge in his pants.

His fingers flexed against the curve of her waist. "Be careful, Beth."

"Why? I'm careful too much." She rubbed her hand against his hard biceps.

"But you aren't in the condition to deliver on the promises your delicious body is making to mine," he whispered in her ear.

He was right, but the instant rejection stung nonetheless. "Oh, look who's got sh-tandards all the shudden."

"Honey, you look near comatose. Any other time..."

His gruff voice sounded far too close to her ear, and she couldn't deny the hot surge of want, but she sure as hell didn't need his help. Determined to make it to her hotel on her own, she pushed away. The move set her off balance, and she stumbled backward. Hank yanked her upright.

"Seems you save damsels in distress even when you're out of your jurisdiction, Sheriff." Ed Webster turned to Beth. "Are you okay?"

Hank twisted to face her senior partner, and heat climbed up Beth's cheeks as she faced the superior smirks on three of the firm's junior partners. Phil Harris, Mason Carter and Charles McMillian chuckled and sipped their bourbon.

"Nice one," Mason said.

Phil slapped Mason on the back. "Yeah, where's your posse, Sheriff?"

"Cut it out, you two." Concern wrinkled Ed's brow. "Do you need some help?"

Ed was the last person Beth wanted to witness her humiliation. Well, make that second-to-last.

Hank effortlessly turned Beth toward the door, moved a hand to the small of her back and guided her forward. "See ya later, Ed."

They wove their way through the throng of people. Hank's large hand pressed firmly against her lower back, bedeviling her nerves and making her knees quake for reasons that had nothing to do with champagne and everything to do with lust.

Dry desert air enveloped Beth after the club's automatic doors swished closed behind them. She staggered to the line for a cab and stumbled into Hank's arms. Her breasts pressed against his wide chest, her head on his shoulder. The woodsy amber scent of his cologne took her back to that summer night before her junior year in college.

His hands had skimmed over her bare skin above her jeans. His kiss had consumed her, a dream come true for the geek who'd worshiped him since she was twelve years old. She'd never forget the *pop, pop, pop* of her button-fly jeans being pulled open. When only one button remained, she'd told him she was a virgin. He'd stopped, telling her that he couldn't do it and adding some bullshit about it being the right thing to do.

Hank pushed her upright. "Just how much did you drink tonight?"

Seeing three of him, she focused on the one in the middle. "Jusss one."

The raised eyebrows on the three Hanks said plainly he didn't believe her.

Beth stomped her foot, the action making her list to one side. "Is true you jig berk." That didn't come out right. "I mean big jerk."

"Uh-huh. Whatever you say." Hank glanced over her shoulder. "OK, here's the cab. Which hotel are you at?"

She blanked out on the hotel's name. Fumbling for a way to describe it, she leaned forward and played with his shirt collar. "Has a fountain and a big, soft bed."

Chapter Ten

The arrival of the yellow cab saved Hank from the mental image of a naked Beth lain out on silk sheets in a huge bed. He poured her lithe frame into the back of the cab and slid in beside her.

Only one hotel on the Las Vegas strip fit her description. "Bellagio, please," he told the driver.

The cabbie winked and pulled out into traffic.

Hank couldn't even hold it against the driver; his mind had fallen into the same gutter. Cars cruised slowly down the street, their shiny exteriors reflecting the neon signs and gigantic billboards featuring the latest shows.

The hotel was at the other end of the strip. Hopefully, that would give them both a few minutes to pull themselves together. And he'd thought it would be a boring night. He'd stopped into the club for a quick beer while Chris and Sam were locked in a high-stakes poker game. When he'd spotted Beth weaving in her seat, he'd been pulled in her direction.

Hank twisted in his seat to face Beth. Normally she never had a hair out of place, but her long brown strands were mussed. He wondered if it felt as soft as it looked. Damn. That was not the road he needed to travel down. "Okay, how many drinks did you really have?"

"Not a liar. Juss one." She held up a single finger. Her middle finger.

Then, in a blink, the annoyed look on her face melted away and she scooted closer. Beth slapped her hand down on his left thigh.

The action stung, but not enough to overpower the desire hardening his cock. *Off limits.* She'd had too much to drink. His body refused to listen to reason as her long fingers massaged his inner thigh, sending jolts of electricity right to his eager cock.

"I don't like you." Her words came out slow and deliberate. "Jus' because you're all muscled and cute does mean I want you... Wait... Don't want you." Her eyes met his and she sucked on her bottom lip for a moment. "Not much."

Her soft words and deft fingers were undoing him. In a last-ditch effort to distract himself from Beth's fingers and the heat threatening to devour him, he looked up into the cab's rearview mirror.

A set of headlights gleamed in the mirror. The cabbie switched lanes. The pair of headlights did the same. When the cab driver moved back into the center lane, so did the car behind them.

Sure, it could be the natural flow of traffic down the strip, but Hank's cop sense went on high alert. He'd only been Dry Creek County Sheriff for six months, but he'd been in law enforcement, military and civilian, since shortly after he blew out his knee playing football his senior year in college. He had almost fifteen years under his belt and he knew to listen to that sixth sense warning him something was wrong.

Leaning forward in his seat, he scanned the glittering surroundings. The blazing lights of the

Little Elvis Wedding Chapel loomed up ahead on a side street. "Can you pull over here?"

The cabbie nodded and swung the car across two lanes of traffic, rounded the corner and came to a stop in front of the chapel.

The chapel stood separated from the street by a wide sidewalk littered with broken bottles and trash but no people. Monday night must not be the day for quickie marriages. A neon profile of Elvis flickered in the window above an open sign. It would do. They'd wait in the lobby to see if anyone stopped.

Hank handed the driver a wad of bills and helped Beth slide out of the car. "Slight detour, then we'll get you to your hotel."

Beth sighed, the dazed look in her eyes obliterating the inquisitive look he normally saw there. "I just want a bed."

The cab driver laughed. "Mazel tov."

He flung the car door shut and tugged Beth into the chapel. The sight that greeted them stopped them in their tracks. Standing side by side, holding hands, they gaped at the shrine they'd entered.

Inside, the lobby was a temple to the king. Huge glossy photos featuring everything from young Elvis wearing a black leather jacket with his hair slicked back to fat Elvis in his white jumpsuit plastered the gold walls. There was just one glaring error in the photographic shrine to the hunka-hunka burning love. The Elvis smiling out from each of the poster-sized pictures couldn't have been more than four feet tall.

"That would explain the 'little' in the Little Elvis Chapel," Hank muttered.

Beth's hand cupped his cock through his pants. "Doesn't feel small." She nipped at his earlobe.

"Mmmm, I've been thinking 'bout what it would be like since that summer. You won't stop this time, right?"

That night was never far from his thoughts. He'd done the right thing and still regretted it to this day.

Light streamed in the windows as a car slammed to a stop in front of the chapel. Looks like it hadn't been only in his head.

Checking the area for exits, he saw only one door. The chapel. He strode over, Beth following along, and pressed his ear to the thin hollow wood.

Hearing muffled laughter, Hank cracked the door open and peeked in. Little Elvis stood at the velvet altar in a spangled jumpsuit officiating the nuptials of a couple, each of whom carried a beer bottle. The exit sign flickered behind Elvis. A way out.

Glancing out the window behind him, he spied two men getting out of a late-model sedan and looking around. No time to wait.

"Come on, we have to go into the wedding chapel." He opened the door wider and pulled her inside.

"Oh, I thought you'd never ask. Did you ask? I don't remember you getting down on one knee." Six feet tall in heels, Beth almost looked him straight in the eye.

"Come on, we've got to get out that door behind Elvis."

The diminutive minister sent a dirty look their way as they snuck up the side of the aisle, but continued with the ceremony.

The bride and groom had eyes only for each other.

He and Beth were a few steps away from the exit when the real Elvis' voice blared through hidden speakers.

"I can't help falling in love with you..."

Little Elvis lowered the music's volume with a remote. "You may now kiss the bride."

Beth stopped moving and jerked Hank to a stop. Stretching, she wound her arms around his neck.

Before he even processed what was about to happen, her lips were on his and his body overruled his better judgment. As soon as her soft, full lips grazed his, Hank forgot who he was. Forgot where he was. Forgot the people who were chasing them. Forgot why Beth was off limits.

Lightning bolts shot through his body when her tongue snuck between his lips and tangled with his. Everything from the neck down turned into heavy, molten want. Her body pressed into him, the thin material of her blue dress taunting him and emphasizing his inability to touch her smooth skin.

Too soon Beth pulled away, grinning vacantly as only the drunk can do. "Let's go have a honeymoon." She led the way out the exit.

Stunned and iron hard, Hank followed her into the grungy hallway, thankful she had the wherewithal to stop. The door clicked shut behind them as they made good on their escape.

Taking one last glance out the one-way window that provided a view of the chapel and part of the lobby, he spotted two men. Dressed in baggy jeans, their faces covered by sunglasses and lowered baseball caps, they didn't look like they were there to get hitched. One looked like a linebacker, tall and square with no discernible neck. The other had an average build, but something about the way he held himself, with a barely reined-in aggression, pegged him as the more dangerous of the two.

The bigger man gestured toward the chapel door and a slow smile spread across his broad face, revealing a gold front tooth. Alarm bells in Hank's head clanged to life. He had no idea what was going on, but he didn't plan on sticking around to find out. Letting go of the doorknob, he grabbed hold of Beth's hand and hurried her down the hall. Turning left, they followed the exit signs through the dark uncarpeted hallway with scuffed walls to a heavy door that opened into the alley.

Holding tightly onto Beth's hand, he tugged her toward the street, pausing as they reached the end of the alley. A quick look around the corner of the building revealed a deserted sidewalk in front of the Little Elvis Wedding Chapel. That meant the men were still inside, probably about to emerge from the same exit he and Beth had used. He wasn't about to wait around to confirm his suspicions.

"Stick with me. We have to get out of here now."

"Whateva you say, husband." Beth giggled, oblivious to the threat about to emerge from the chapel.

He hailed a passing cab and climbed inside after Beth, keeping his body between her and the chapel door. "The Palms. We're in a hurry."

"Yeah, I felt the same way after each one of my weddings." The female driver chuckled in the front seat and merged with traffic.

For once when he sat next to Beth, tension rather than lust locked his muscles tight. He didn't know why those guys were following them, but something bad was going down.

No way could he leave Beth alone at her hotel. She was coming back with him and he was going to find out what the hell was going on.

Chapter Eleven

*W*ho's following you and why?" Hank watched as Beth tossed her glasses on the nightstand and flopped onto the king-size bed in his hotel room, wishing like hell he could join her.

Her brown hair fanned outward, contrasting with the crisp white of the comforter. It reminded him of a black-and-white cookie, but it wasn't his stomach that was hungry for her. He shifted uncomfortably, trying to give his hard dick some more room in his black trousers.

"The only man following me is you, all the way from Dry Creek just to marry me. How romantic." Beth giggled and extended one long leg his way, revealing a mind-boggling amount of upper thigh.

On her foot was some type of impossibly high-heeled shoe. She pointed the opened-toed red shoe at him, revealing glittery, hot-pink-painted toenails. "A little help pleash, hubby."

Pulled forward like a deer to a saltlick, he grasped her ankle and went to work on the thin strap of material circling it. "We're not married."

"You're so funny."

"Answer the question. Who's following you?"

"Your fingers feel so good."

Fuck. Staring down at the long leg in his grasp, he accepted that he wasn't going to get any information out of her right now. He marveled at the smoothness of her leg and the strong calf muscle hidden underneath her soft skin that flexed as she rotated her foot. His cock twitched in response.

She hiccupped twice before giggling again.

"So how much did you really have to drink tonight?" Fumbling to unhook the strap, he tried to get his body to calm down. Hank gritted his teeth and recited the Miranda Rights in his head because if anyone needed that warning right now, it was him.

"Only one glash. I don't like to drink." Laid out on the bed, Beth arched her back and stretched her willowy arms toward the wine-colored fabric headboard. A soft moan escaped as she extended her upper body.

White-hot desire ripped through Hank's body as suddenly as a thunder clap. If there was a reason why he shouldn't sink down to his knees and run his hands up her supple thighs, he sure as hell didn't remember it. The shoe dropped from her foot. He stared at the high arch curving upward from her sole and fought to remember why this was wrong.

Beth sat up, pulling her foot from his grasp. "Claire and I are sishters now." She clapped her hands and giggled. "That's awesome!"

Yeah. That's why Beth was off limits. She was his sister's best friend and she was blasted out of her mind. So while there was nothing more he'd like to do than strip her down and fuck her silly, he couldn't do it.

"We did not get married." He took a step back from the bed and the possibilities it provided.

"That's not nice." Beth raised her other leg. "I have one more shoe, then you can help me get my dresh off."

Hank's insubordinate cock jumped at the idea. If he looked in the mirror right now, he was afraid he'd see a bug-eyed, panting, cartoon-style caricature of himself. Furious at his reaction, he grabbed her ankle and yanked off her shoe without undoing the strap. "Time to sober you up. Come on, in the shower you go."

She grinned wickedly. "I'll scrub your back if you scrub mine." Her hand traveled up her right leg, disappeared under the hem of her dress and stopped just short of her pussy. "Unless you'd rather just watch."

Blood rushed south from his brain and his balls tightened immediately.

Her fingers danced underneath her dress, tormenting him with mental images of her sneaking a finger into her panties. The unknown tormented him. Thong? Bikini? Lace? Satin? Was she slick already, waiting for him to bury himself deep within her?

Another soft moan sent his blood pressure through the roof as she arched her back off the thick comforter. "My favorite thing to think about when I touch my clit is you going down on me, licking your way around my wet pussy." Her fingers sped up their undercover rotations. "As soon as I saw you with that beard I wanted to feel it scratching against my inner thighs as I came."

Hypnotized by the sight before him and entranced by her soft alto voice, the hotel could have burned down around them and Hank wouldn't have been able to move from that spot.

"Do you want to taste me, Hank?" Beth withdrew her hand from underneath her dress, holding two fingers apart from the rest. Bringing her hand up to her mouth, her pink tongue slowly slid up one side of her middle finger before she sucked it into her hot mouth. Millimeter by millimeter she pulled it from her glistening red lips. "Because I taste good."

Hank looked at the pointer finger, wet with her own juices, that she held out to him. For the first time since he'd been a teen, he worried about coming in his pants. Fuck, what this woman did to him. He took an unsteady step forward until his shins banged against the bed frame.

She grabbed his pants and made quick work of his belt. "That's it, come give your wife what she needs."

Effective as a bucket of ice dropped down his boxers, her words froze his hot lust.

Pulling Beth up from the bed, he pushed her toward the bathroom. "We. Are. Not. Married." Speaking those words hurt more than they should.

"Whatever you shay, honey."

Once inside the marble-covered room, he busied himself with getting the water ready while she hung back in the doorway. A cold shower would jolt her out of her intoxication.

He yanked open the glass door and twisted the water knob all the way to the blue side. Maybe later he'd get a chance to take one too. God knew he needed it. The water rushed out of the large, round showerhead, splashing against the bottom of the gray marble floor.

Closing the door, he snatched a towel from the shelf and wiped his hands. "Okay, it's ready. Why don't you…"

As soon as he turned around, the words died in his mouth.

Beth stood in the doorway wearing nothing but a sheer black bra and lacy panties.

Gripping the cool marble countertop to steady himself, he took in a fortifying breath. What he *couldn't* do was pry his eyes from her.

Five feet, nine inches tall in her bare feet, she had legs that went on forever. They weren't sticks either. No. She had the strong, limber legs of a woman who embraced the power of her body. His gaze traveled upward over her narrow hips and flat stomach. He spotted a tattoo started above her right hipbone and went up her rib cage: a golden phoenix. The crisp detail and vivid colors of the yellow-and-orange bird with its wings spread as if about to take flight attested to the amount of time and money involved in getting the tattoo. If he ever figured out how to form words again, he'd have to ask her about it.

Her small, round breasts were veiled behind the see-through lace of her black bra but her dark-brown nipples, puckered into hard points, extended outward, calling him and pulling him closer. Two simple gold rings hung from a silver necklace fastened around her long neck.

He remembered the rings from that summer night so long ago. Her parents' wedding rings. She never took them off. That and an unbuttoned pair of jeans were all she'd worn when she'd lain back on the plaid picnic blanket. Barely twenty, she'd found him alone at Lake Harvey with a six pack of cheap beer, nursing his wounds from yet another breakup with Amanda in their on-again, off-again premarital downward spiral.

He'd been looking for a soft landing. She'd deserved more. He'd stopped them just in time, telling her it was the right thing to do. The same thing he needed to do tonight.

Mind and body fighting each other, he clung to the countertop, its rough underside scratching his fingertips. The pain acted as a poor distraction from the sexual wanting nearly overpowering him.

"I'm not a virgin this time," Beth whispered. "Your honor isn't in question." She walked to him, swaying only a bit, and wrapped her arms around his neck. Her lips covered his with hungry little kisses. "Turn off the shower."

Conflicted beyond reasoning, Hank wanted to scream out in frustration. Her tight body pressed against his, her fingers were running through his hair. When she curled one lean leg around his hip, her heel touching the small of his back and the heat from her lace-covered pussy warming his cock that strained against his zipper, his self-control shattered.

Ignoring the running shower, he lifted her up so both of her legs wrapped around his waist.

Murmuring her approval, she nipped his earlobe then sucked it before trailing kisses down his neck. "Bed now, Hank, or I'm going to fuck you against that cold shower door."

That wouldn't do. He wanted space to spread her long, flexible legs to better taste her slick center. That would be only the beginning. He planned on spending the hours until dawn making her toes curl. Repeatedly.

Surrendering to the madness, he strode out of the bathroom carrying her toward the bed on the opposite side of the room. They made it as far as the chaise lounge. He sat down on the edge and Beth's legs came down from around his waist.

On her knees astride him, she raised herself up until her tits filled his line of sight. "Touch me, Hank."

He dragged a finger across the lace of her black bra, male pride ballooning as her nipples tightened beneath the sheer material. His fingers itched to stroke those nubs, but he held back. "Where do you want me to touch you?"

Her answer was to move so her taut nipple was only a hairsbreadth from his hungry mouth. "My nipples. Pull on them."

Pushing down the dark straps until her bare breasts were freed, he took a brown nipple in his mouth, sucking it lightly, wary of hurting her delicate skin. He pulled away to lick from the nub to the outside of her dark areola and she shuddered in his arms.

Her fingers dug into the muscles in his shoulders. "Harder."

Fuck. His tight balls straddled the pleasure/pain tightrope. Her half groan, half plea almost sent him over the edge into oblivion. Fighting to regain some control, he took a deep breath, inhaling vanilla mixed with her own musky scent. As he tugged on one nipple with his teeth, he grasped the other between two fingers, rolling it counterclockwise.

"Yes." She moaned the word into the darkness and ground her body against him. "Fuck, that's good."

Damn straight it was. Every part of him felt electric. His body was strung tighter than a bow, hard everywhere. He needed release in her soft body.

Letting go of her nipples, he turned his face up to hers and their mouths met. Her sweet tongue curled around his as he deepened the kiss. Palming her ass, he kept her anchored to his erection as they devoured each other. Pleasure spiraled upward when she rubbed her wet core against him. He wanted her more than he'd ever wanted anyone in his life.

Finally, he admitted to himself that he'd been waiting since that summer night to touch her, to feel her pussy clench around his cock as she orgasmed.

Shooting up from the chaise lounge, he carried her to the bed, again knocking his shins against the bed frame, but the pain barely registered. He turned and sat on the bed before falling back with Beth on top of him. Her lips never left his but it seemed as if her hands were everywhere, as were his. Rubbing. Caressing. Stroking. Unable to take it any longer, he rolled her off of him and stood up.

Beth stared at him with hooded eyes that promised sexual nirvana beyond all expectations. Driven by a primal need, he pulled his shirt over his head, buttons flying across the room, and flipped off his black dress shoes. Looking down, he unbuttoned his slacks and let them fall the floor. Thumbs hooked in his boxer's waistband, he glanced up.

Beth was curled onto her side, eyes closed, breathing deeply.

Aching with need, Hank stared. Everything about her that had been tense with want had softened and become pliant. He sat down beside her on the bed and stroked her smooth hair. It was as soft as he'd imagined.

The realization of what he'd almost done washed over him. Shame and regret settled in his stomach like a weight. Where had his honor been? She'd saved them this time. How could he have considered having sex with Beth when she'd drunk so much? He wanted to kick himself for what he'd almost done. Instead, he covered Beth with the comforter, tucking a corner underneath her chin, and got up from the bed.

She snuggled deeper into the fluffy whiteness. "Love you, baby. I always have." A slight smile curled her kiss-swollen lips.

Yeah, she loved him all right. Tonight she loved him, champagne and tacky wedding chapels. In the morning she'd be hard-pressed to decide which one she hated more.

Hank plucked his clothes from the floor and flung them into a nearby chair. He rescued damsels in distress, as Webster had said earlier tonight. Ha. From the looks of things, they needed to be rescued from *him*.

Pissed off at himself, he marched to the bathroom and the waiting cold shower.

Chapter Twelve

*B*eth, eyelids still sleep-heavy, burrowed into the heavy warmth wrapped around her. She'd never slept so well in her whole life. She'd dreamed of getting a massage in the middle of a sultry island paradise. Lots of palm trees, a soft breeze and warm hands all over her body. She had to figure out what kind of mattress this was so she could order one for home.

Five more minutes of snooze time, then it was on to the shower and another day of estate law seminars. She rolled over onto her stomach, only to be pulled back onto her side and dragged against the source of all the toasty heat.

Her eyes snapped open and fear lodged in her throat. This wasn't her hotel room.

Body frozen in panic, she flicked her gaze downward.

A man's hand cupped her breast, the necklace with her parents' wedding rings twisted around his fingers.

Holding her breath, she realized her butt lay nestled against someone's morning wood.

Heart thundering inside her chest, she inched her head around to get a peek at the man whose bed she shared. Her foul morning breath whooshed out of her mouth when she came nose to nose with Hank.

Oh shit.

"Go back to sleep, darlin'. We're on vacation," he mumbled in a horse, half-asleep voice.

Turning her head away from him, she stared at the thumb only a millimeter away from her fast-hardening nipple. This was not good. Not good at all.

Desperate to understand how all of this had happened, Beth rewound the previous night in her head. She'd gone out to dinner with other conference attendees, where she'd had ginger ale. After dinner they'd gone to a club at one of the other hotels on the strip. She'd had a glass of champagne. Only one. Always only one. Everyone else ordered martinis. That's when things got jumbled up in her mind.

She remembered everything had felt funny and her desperation to go back to her hotel room. Then Hank had appeared by her side. There was a cab. Elvis had shown up. A very short Elvis.

What had happened with Elvis? Oh yeah, Elvis had told Hank to kiss the bride and he'd turned and kissed her.

Ice spread through her veins. *Dear sweet baby Jesus.*

Unable to move anything else, she blinked her eyes. Fast. Her lungs began to ache, reminding her she needed to breathe. Gasping for air, she bolted upright.

"Good morning," Hank drawled as he rubbed the bridge of his nose. "How are you feeling?"

Despite the fact that he'd held one of her boobs only minutes before, Beth reflexively grabbed the white sheet, pulled it up to her neck and kept her gaze locked on the maroon-and-gold striped wallpaper. "Fine and dandy. Perfect. Never better."

She slapped her hand over her mouth to shut herself up.

"Yeah? Good because you were in rare form last night."

Rare form? What had she done that could be worse than marrying him? Looking down, she didn't see a ring on her left finger. She let out a sigh of relief. But the feeling was momentary because in the same moment realization dawned that she was wearing only her panties.

In bed.

With Hank.

"What happened?"

He laughed, a low rumbling that made her stomach do triple flips and turned her body to jelly. She didn't want to turn back and look at the source of that bone-melting sound. But running at full speed out the door wasn't an option, especially since her dress was hidden somewhere in this room. At least she hoped so.

Curling her knees to her chest, she looked over her shoulder at him. "Hank, tell me right now what happened."

The bastard had the audacity to wink at her from beneath his chestnut hair. Damn her wandering eyes, she couldn't help but look lower to his bare broad shoulders and his muscular chest covered in darker brown hair, which narrowed as it traveled south. Lounging against the pillows, clad only in black cotton boxer briefs, his long and thick salute to a new day stood at full mast in his lap.

If she'd gotten to enjoy that last night and didn't remember, she sure as hell was going to be pissed off.

Hank cleared his throat, drawing her gaze upward.

"My eyes are up here you know." He wriggled his eyebrows at her and a wicked grin spread across his face.

Her stomach dropped to her toes. She was a respectable, boring estate attorney who lived in a small town in Nebraska. She didn't have sex on the first date, let alone drunkenly marry her best friend's brother. The same brother who'd refused to be her first lover, saying he didn't have sex with virgins. Embarrassment burned her cheeks.

"Um, did we..." She waved a hand over the bed, unable to bring herself to say the words.

"I'll leave it to your imagination while I go take a shower."

He curled forward and dropped a quick peck on top of her head before getting out of bed. After a quick full-body stretch that showed off every muscle in his toned back, he strutted to the bathroom, his form-fitting boxers highlighting his hard ass in all its glory.

Squeezing the soft sheets in her fists, Beth managed not to move until the bathroom door clicked shut. She waited a beat then tumbled out of the bed, hampered by the sheets twisted around her bare legs.

Frantic to get the hell out of there before he got out of the bathroom, she searched the room for her dress. When she heard the shower turn on a few minutes later, she had to concede defeat. Neither her dress nor purse was there. No cell. No hotel key. No money. What in the hell was she going to do now?

Needing a clearer head than hers, she reached for the room phone. Fingers shaking, she dialed

Claire's cell. Together, they'd figure out what to do next.

It took forever for Claire to pick up.

"Hello?"

"Claire, I think I'm in trouble." Panic tightened Beth's voice as she gripped the phone receiver.

"Where are you? What's happened?" Claire hollered over the sound of beeping and revving motors.

"I'm still in Vegas." Beth couldn't think of how to break the news to her best friend. Where should she start?

"What's wrong? Did you gamble away your hotel money? Do you need bail? What is it?"

"Oh shit, Claire," she mumbled.

The blaring horn of a truck sounded over the line. "What? I can't hear you, Beth. Speak up!"

"I can't talk louder. He's in the bathroom. I had to wait for the shower to come on before I could call you." She tried to rein in the nervousness playing havoc on her mind.

"Who's in the shower? Who's he?"

Taking a deep breath, she steeled herself. The best solution was to put it all out there. "Claire, I think I married your brother."

"What?"

Beth yanked the receiver away from her ear, ringing from the hollered question. The sound of running water stopped. She gulped and twisted the phone cord in her hand. "Oh God, the shower just turned off. What am I going to do?" Apprehension vibrated through her tense body.

"Beth, which brother?" Claire screamed into the phone.

Hunching over the phone, she whispered, "Hank. I think I married Hank."

The bathroom door opened, releasing a cloud of steam.

"Who you talking to?" Hank strolled out, a towel slung around his hips.

Flashing him a tight smile, she dropped the phone receiver onto the cradle. "Uh, no one. Room service, but I changed my mind."

"Uh-huh." Hank wandered back into the bathroom.

Flopping back onto the bed, she tried to figure out how she'd get herself out of this mess.

တတတ

As much fun as it was to see Beth squirming, Hank had to tell her they weren't married. It wasn't going to be pretty. Not that pretty was a word she inspired right now. He wasn't sure if the green-around-the-gills look was from the idea of having him as a husband or the after-effects of her night out on the town. Either way, she looked like hell, with her hair shooting out in all directions and some black goop dotting the underside of her eyes.

So why did he still feel like tumbling her over and burying his face in that rat's nest on top of her head?

Giving in to the inevitable, Hank grabbed her dress from where it had fallen behind the chaise lounge and tossed it to her. "We're not married."

Hope lit her eyes. "We're not?" Beth jumped up from the bed and wiggled her lace-clad ass in celebration.

Damn, what was he, some kind of an ogre?

Annoyed with her obvious relief, Hank grumbled to himself. "Women."

"Okay, so if we're not married, did I just dream about a really short Elvis?" The smooth material of her dress muffled her words as she pulled it over her head.

Hank's spidey sense pulsated. Something was going on beyond the few verbal threats she'd told him about the other day. The truth of it crawled up his spine, sending off sparks of suspicion. "You sure you only had one drink last night?"

"You know what happened to my parents with the drunk driver. My limit has always been one." She secured the leather belt around her waist, pulling the material tightly closed. Her fingers stilled and she looked up, fear darkening her eyes. "Do you think someone slipped something into my drink?"

The idea made sense. It explained why Beth had been so out of it. But it didn't account for the two guys who'd followed them into the chapel. The more he thought about it, the more certain he was she'd been targeted last night.

He sat down beside her on the bed. "Any idea why someone would have slipped you something and then followed you?"

Her face blanched. Her gaze fell to her lap, where her hands twisted the silk of her dress into a knot of worry.

"What aren't you telling me, Beth?"

She turned her dark-brown eyes toward him. Flecks of gold in her irises shimmered with unshed tears. "It's probably nothing, but you know someone is buying up the land around my grandparents' house? They'll only buy if everyone agrees to sell. I'm the last holdout."

Understanding dawned. The Lakota casino was set to open up next year in Council County. The tribe announced the casino would go near the Highway Five entrance to the reservation, but it hadn't been finalized yet.

"You know, a lot of folks don't believe the casino will go where the tribe announced. According to town gossip, plenty of people were gambling millions on land that may or may not lead to the new casino." He strode to her side. "Whoever guesses right stands to make a fortune. Hotels, restaurants and other auxiliary businesses would pay top dollar to locate near the casino."

With that kind of money at stake, Beth was playing a dangerous game without backup.

Hank wrapped an arm around her shoulder and hugged her closer. "So that explains why you've been getting threats. Has anyone threatened you to your face?"

She snorted into his shoulder. "Mrs. Cranston said she'd always known you couldn't trust a Mexican to do the right thing."

"Mrs. Cranston is an ignorant old bag who'd better hope she doesn't get caught speeding in Dry Creek County."

Chuckling darkly, Beth pushed away from him. "Thanks." She stood and started pacing, her bare feet leaving indentions in the plush carpet. "I've gotten some nasty anonymous phone calls and texts. Someone vandalized the house."

He jumped up from the bed and grabbed her elbow, forcing her to stop pacing. "What?"

She kept her face averted. "Yeah, the day my car conked out for the billionth time, but nothing too bad. Some broken windows and spray-painted walls."

Anger burbled inside of him, making his gut clench. "Why didn't you tell me when I gave you a ride home?"

"The house is just over the border in Council County. I reported it to Sheriff Wilcox. He said it was probably just kids partying in an abandoned house."

He just bet the lazy, corrupt son of a bitch did think that. "So what's he going to do about it?"

"Nothing. Oh, he says he'll look into the threats, but nothing ever happens." She wrapped around her chest, her hands rubbing her upper arms. "He suggested I sell."

"There must be a stream of stupid flowing into Council County's water supply."

"Yeah, now you understand why I live in Dry Creek." She smiled wanly at her tepid joke.

"Not that I want you to sell, but why haven't you?"

"My grandfather built that house. He'd work a twelve-hour shift in the slaughterhouse and then turn around and spend his off hours building the house. It took him ten years to complete it. Sure, it's an ugly house, but it's my only tie to my family. It's all I have left of them." A single tear slid over one high cheekbone, but fire burned in her gaze. "I won't sell. Ever."

Now family, *that* he could understand.

"Okay. So tell me about last night." He wanted to pull her into his arms, but she looked as skittish as a calf on branding day.

"I went to dinner with other conference speakers and attendees. We had reservations for a table at one of the hotel clubs, so we went there. I had a glass of pop at dinner, a champagne at the club, and then everything went fuzzy."

"Anyone from home with you?"

"At the dinner, most everyone was from the firm. At the club there were several people from home. A few were already at the club when we got there." She clutched a fist to her stomach. "Could the drug still be in my system?"

He was going to enjoy the feel of his fist crushing the jaw of whoever did this. "It's unlikely. Your symptoms sound like it was GHB or Rohypnol, and both tend not to leave trace evidence behind."

She sank down to the chaise lounge, her normal latte complexion ashen. "Great. So there's no way to prove it."

Hank shook his head. "Not likely." The fact that he was impotent to do more than offer advice rankled him.

Beth threw up her hands, stormed over to her shoes and swiped them off the floor before flopping down onto a stiff desk chair. Stuffing her feet inside each high heel, she tucked her mussed hair behind her ears. She leaned forward and fastened the delicate straps around her tiny ankles. The move accentuated her long neck.

Assaulted by unbidden visions of sucking on her earlobe and trailing hot kisses down the tender column of her throat, Hank sucked in a deep breath.

This was not the time for that. "We need to report this to the local police."

Anger snapped in her gaze when she leveled those brown eyes on him. "Hell no."

"Don't be stupid."

"You know what's stupid? Turning to law enforcement with a story that I may have been drugged, but can't prove it and anyway nothing bad happened." She rose to her full height. Her aggressive stance emphasized by the hands on her hips. "I think the Las Vegas Police Department has more pressing things to take care of and so do I. The conference panel I'm on begins in three hours, and I still need to finalize my Power Point." She held out her hand to him, palm up toward the ceiling. "So give me my purse."

She hadn't told him about how many threats there had been or the vandalism.

She'd danced a jig when she'd found out they weren't married.

She was acting like a stubborn fool about being drugged.

He should warn her not to let the door hit her on the ass on her way out.

But he couldn't.

He may have been so blinded by lust last night that he forgot about his honor, but not now. Too many signs warned of danger ahead. He reached between the mattress and box spring, pulled out her small black purse and held it out.

Eyeing him warily, she crossed the room and grabbed the purse. Her gaze narrowed when he wouldn't surrender it to her. "What now?"

"Your thing's in three hours?"

"Yeah." She tugged at the purse.

Laying on his best aw-shucks charm, he kept the purse locked in his grasp. "What a coincidence. I've been hoping to learn more about estate planning. We'll take a cab to your hotel so you can finish up and then head over to the conference together."

"Really?" She was giving him her best you're-full-of-shit look. "Isn't that convenient."

"I agree. So, you'll give me a couple of minutes?"

"Look, Hank, I appreciate you coming to my rescue last night. Really, I do. But I'm fine today and I can take care of myself." She yanked on the purse to no avail.

He let all pretense fall from his face. "No. There were two guys following you."

Her mouth tightened and fear flashed in her eyes before disappearing. "Probably just wolves thinking they'd found a drunk and helpless sheep." Releasing the purse, she stepped back. "Hank, thank you for your help last night but this isn't your battle."

Ouch. That hurt like a jab to the nose. "So you say."

"Why are you doing this?" She crossed her arms and probably would have shot laser beams from her eyes at him if it was possible.

"It's the right thing to do." Tucking the purse under an arm, he headed toward the bathroom to gather his shaving gear.

"Where have I heard that high-minded phrase before?"

He shut the door against her question, knowing those words had changed their lives on a hot summer night a long time ago—and they were about to do it again.

Chapter Thirteen

$\mathcal{S}$o, how many of your neighbors are pissed off at you for not selling?" Hank's disembodied voice filtered through the closed bathroom door in Beth's hotel room.

She wrapped the blow dryer's twisted cord around its handle and stuffed it into the basket under the sink. "Most, but I can't imagine any of them are behind this." No, the worst she'd gotten were a few dirty looks and snide comments whispered behind her back.

"Me neither. Mrs. Cranston is a royal bitch, but she doesn't hit me as the type to get her hands dirty like this."

She tried to picture the brittle, thin eighty-year-old Mrs. Cranston in a black ski mask spraying graffiti and tossing hamburger wrappers around Beth's grandparents' house. If the situation hadn't been so serious, the image would have made her laugh.

She'd known her neighbors for most of her life, ever since she'd gone to live with her grandparents. It didn't make sense that any of them would do this. She even worked with Mrs. Hunihan, who lived a few miles up the road, and hadn't noticed any difference in the way the executive secretary acted toward her. What motive would there be? Money, sure, but even as ticked off as some of them were, they weren't violent folks.

"That leaves the buyer." His voice sounded stronger, he must have moved closer to the door.

Turning, she gazed at the closed door, picturing him on the other side in his jeans and lightweight gray dress shirt. Sitting next to him in the taxi on the way over here had been torture. She'd tried to stay on her side of the seat, but he'd felt no such compulsion and her skin sizzled from his nearness. Excitement bounced around her stomach at the memory and she laid her palm against the door to steady herself.

What was wrong with her? She had to distance herself from him before it was too late, but with who knows who after her, she wasn't going to get rid of him anytime soon.

She slipped her black, knee-length dress from the hanger on the bathroom door, lowered the back zipper and stepped inside it.

"You haven't been able to get any more information about who it is?"

Raising the dress up, she slid her arms into the cap sleeves then cracked open the door, hoping to see him on the other side. No such luck. "Nope, all roads lead to a farmer who has been dead for a decade."

"Damn, what I'd give to have access to my computer right now."

"You can't log in from mine?"

"No, we have a closed system that only allows certain IP addresses access."

Beth wriggled inside the dress, one arm stretched behind her back, trying to reach the zipper.

114

Her fingers brushed the metal zipper pull, but couldn't grasp it enough to yank it up. Hunching over, she inched the fabric higher until she reached the zipper. She grunted and jerked it upward until it snagged on something and wouldn't go any higher.

Shit. Shit. Shit.

Tugging it harder was an exercise in futility, but she tried anyway. Her shoulder ached from the awkward position and her glasses had slipped down her nose so far they were in danger of dropping off and smashing to the floor. Having to show up late to the conference with her only pair of glasses held together by a piece of tape was the last thing her career needed right now. Admitting defeat, she stood and adjusted her glasses. The world came back into focus with Hank standing in the now completely open bathroom door.

"Need help?"

A childish part of her wanted to say no, but who was she trying to fool? She needed Hank for more than just the zipper. "Yes, thank you."

Beth turned her back to give him access to the trouble spot. Goose bumps prickled her skin when his hands touched the small of her back, his thumb resting against the curve of her ass. Unable to stop herself, she shivered.

He didn't say a word.

She couldn't, even if she were able to form a single thought at the moment.

Instead, she closed her eyes when he tried to pull the stubborn zipper higher, only to have the smooth material of her dress slide up her bare thighs.

He cleared his throat. "Um...looks like I...uh...need to pull it down first."

She peeked at his reflection in the mirror. He concentrated on the zipper as if the fate of the world were at stake. His hands shook as he lowered the zipper to the middle of her back and hesitated, staring at the expanse of skin on display, before sliding it ever so slowly upward. When he reached the top, he took a step back, flexing his hand as if it had been stung. His gaze met hers in the mirror and neither moved.

Possibilities hung heavy in the electrified air, constricting her chest and scaring her down to her hot-pink toenails. Hank looked at her as if she could be the best thing to ever happen to him. Like she was perfect. Like he loved her.

"Beth." He whispered her name, his tone a combination of plea and promise.

Staring at the reflection of his hazel eyes in the mirror and seeing the hope they held sent reality crashing down on her.

Amanda had twisted him into knots promising they'd start a family, after they bought the boat or the house or the dream vacation. But she'd always changed her mind. He'd confessed to Claire that not having a family wasn't the only reason for the divorce, but it was a big one.

She loved him too much to put him through that again.

The realization hit her like a slap to the face. How she'd called love lust for so long, she had no idea. She loved him. Always had. Her throat tightened with regret for all the things lost before they were realized.

If they ever got serious, she'd have to tell him she couldn't have kids, make him choose between her and family. Family meant everything to both of them and she was destined not to have one—at least not one of her own blood. She wouldn't force that fate on him when she knew just how much his family line meant to him. Blinking away the tears flooding her eyes, she swallowed past the lump in her throat.

Doing the right thing hurt like a bitch.

"Thanks for your help." She smiled weakly at his reflection. "We'd better get a move on."

Confusion and hurt flashed across his face before he squared his jaw and nodded at her. "Yeah, of course. I'll wait for you in the lobby."

Without pausing for a response, he spun on his heel and strode out the door. A second later the hotel room door clicked shut.

Beth sank down on the edge of the tub. Shaking like a loose roof shingle in a tornado, she gasped for breath as her heart exploded into a million sharp, jagged pieces.

ৎঌৎঌৎঌ

Fifteen minutes later, Beth had to fight the urge to sneak back into the elevator when she saw Hank standing alone by the hotel's rotating front door. Her body ached like she had the twenty-four hour flu and she had the nausea to go with it. Nothing like realizing you loved the wrong man to make you wish you could curl up into a ball and never get out of bed.

A woman tugging a screaming toddler stopped next to her at the elevator bank. The bawling child's misery drew Hank's attention her way. The ice in his gaze did nothing to melt the heat flooding her body at the mere sight of him. Sighing, she trudged toward him. This was the path she'd chosen, she'd just have to push her way through it. Maybe in a few days, it wouldn't hurt so much.

Hell, she might as well admit it would more likely be decades before that happened.

The Nebraska football fight song blaring out of his jeans pocket saved her from having to make small talk. Without acknowledging her, he pushed his way through the rotating door, obviously assuming, correctly as it turned out, that she'd follow.

Back ramrod straight, he stood perfectly still and didn't even make a flicker of a movement toward his phone when it started ringing again. For as long as she'd known him, he'd been unable to let a phone ring. The Layton family curiosity would drive him to pick it up, but not this time. The vein near his temple bulged as he ground his teeth throughout the thirty-second jingle. If he kept this up, he wasn't going to have any molars left. Pissed off didn't begin to describe him.

As for her, she felt like shit. It had taken ten minutes of deep breathing and pacing before she could get her emotions under control. Now they were waiting in the taxi line and her gut twisted with anxiety. She yearned to say something to make him feel better, let him know that it wasn't him, but before she could open her mouth, the fight song went off in his pants again.

"You gonna get that?"

He kept staring at the back of the sixty-ish valet's shaved head. "Nope."

"Look, Hank—"

"Save it Beth, okay?" He turned and glared at her, tension streaming from his tightly wound body. "We're friends, but you won't even trust me to help you when someone's threatening you. You kiss me, but then you pretend there's nothing between us. I spent too many years with a master manipulator who turned me inside out every chance she got to ever go down that path again. From now on, you're just my little sister's best friend who happens to be in trouble. I'm with you until we find out who's behind the threats, but don't expect me to act like nothing's changed. I'm done chasing you when you obviously don't want to be caught."

And she thought she couldn't feel any worse.

Dropping her chin to her chest to hide her watery eyes, she fought to regain her tenuous hold on her emotions and bite back the apology ready to spill out of her mouth. No. This was for the best. She could do this. She had to do this.

"Your cab." The valet's soft voice contrasted with the dirty look he leveled at Hank. Opening the door, he smiled warmly at Beth.

When Hank didn't move, she walked toward the cab's open door. "Thank you."

"Arriba los corazones," the valet said as she slid across the cab's backseat.

Hank sat down next to her, shutting the door after him. "What was that all about?"

"I think he was trying to be nice."

"Oh yeah? What did he say?"

Beth shrugged. "I know a few phrases and words, but I don't speak Spanish. My grandparents were pretty firm in their desire to raise an All-American girl. They thought it would give me the same advantages as the white kids."

Of course, now one of her biggest hobbies was genealogy and she'd signed up for Spanish classes at the local community college. The reminder of her grandparents laid a heavy weight on her shoulders.

What would they think of how she'd turned out? The fact that she was an attorney, was it proof they'd made the right choices? How did you ever know?

Weariness settled into her bones as she contemplated the uncertainty of it all. Needing a distraction, she grabbed her phone and turned it on, not taking her eyes off the small screen while it powered up.

"Where to?" the driver asked.

"Paris."

"Oui, oui." The cabbie chuckled at his joke.

Hank busied himself with his phone, a deep worry line denting his forehead. She was about to ask what the trouble was when the jingle of her own phone announced it was ready.

The blinking red message light at the top of her cell flashed like crazy. Between taking a shower, getting ready and finishing her Power Point, she'd received forty-five texts.

CLAIRE: WHAT HAPPENED? U OK?

CLAIRE: ARE WE SISTERS? SO EXCITED!!!!

CLAIRE: WHAT'S GOING ON? UR NOT ANSWERING.

CLAIRE: U AND HANK GETTING IT ON? :)

CLAIRE: THAT WAS A JOKE!

CLAIRE: OOPS, JUST TALKED 2 MOM AND IT SLIPPED OUT. KINDA SORTA ON PURPOSE. DON'T HATE.

UNKNOWN: YOUNG LADY, DID YOU ELOPE WITH MY SON? MAKE HIM ANSWER HIS PHONE. I HAVE CALLED TWELVE TIMES. HE IS NOT TOO BIG FOR ME TO STRAIGHTEN OUT.

CLAIRE: CALL ME IF UR NOT ON UR WAY TO TAHITI.

Her fingers hesitated over the tiny keyboard. What to say? That she made a massive fool of herself with Hank? Again? No, that just sounded pathetic. That she'd probably been drugged by God-knows-who? Not unless she wanted the entire Layton clan to descend upon Vegas en masse. That she wished Little Elvis had pronounced them husband and wife? Definitely no. Just the thought made her body as jittery as the time she ate an entire bag full of chocolate-covered espresso beans.

Forget it. She'd call later. Firmly, she shoved the phone into her briefcase. It took all of three heart beats for the second thoughts to come rushing in. This was not a conversation she wanted to have via text, but she couldn't not respond. Knowing Claire, if she didn't answer soon, her best friend would be on the first flight to Vegas. She pulled the phone out and started typing with her thumbs.

BETH: AM OK. NOT MARRIED. EXPLAIN LATER.

After hitting send, she slid her finger across the screen until Hank's mother's text appeared. Glenda Layton was not someone to toy with. When it came to her children and getting them married off, the woman was a five foot, eight inch Pit Bull with an attitude problem. No way was she explaining this fiasco to Glenda. That little bit of heaven was all Hank's.

"You need to call your mom."

"Yeah, she left me a million messages." He ran his hands through his brown hair, leaving tufts of it sticking straight up. "She even texted. I didn't think she knew how to do that."

"What are you going to say?"

The giant Eiffel Tower gleamed up ahead. The driver zipped the car over to the right-hand lane and turned his blinker on. The click, click of it echoed in the silence after her question.

Hank sighed and sank back into his seat. "You know my mom, there's nothing I can tell her. Knowing her, she'll have dug up every bit of gossip from the last six months, scoured the online marriage certificates in Vegas, gotten every little piece of information out of my brothers—that is, if Chris and Sam are out of their poker game yet—and made contact with a private eye."

The description made her laugh. "She does always seem to know everything about everything."

The light bulb went off in Beth's head as bright as the sun. Why hadn't they thought of it earlier? She opened her mouth, but Hank cut her off before she could utter a word.

"I'm already on it. I'll text her now and call her after I have a chat with Little Elvis. With any luck, he'll be willing to share his surveillance video from last night." His large fingers crawled across his phone, too big to type quickly on the tiny keyboard keys. "Mom will give me all the rumors and innuendo there is about who wants to buy your grandparents' house."

Chapter Fourteen

$\mathcal{H}$er perfume filled the cab with its warm, inviting scent until all Hank wanted to do was bury his face in the soft curve of her neck and breathe in his fill. This was torture; pure, blissful torture, and if he wasn't so pissed off, he'd be in heaven. The need to touch her wreaked havoc on his ability to function, let alone compose a decent text to his mom that wouldn't send her through the roof.

Mentally groaning, Hank hit the itty-bitty delete key on his phone. Again. He hated texting. If God had wanted man to text, He would have made the keyboard bigger.

HANK: DON'T KNOW WHAT CLAIRE SAID, BUT NOT MARRIED. ALL WELL HERE. HOPE YOU ARE GOOD. TALK TO YOU SOON. LOVE HANK.

Giving the message another look, his finger hovered over the delete key. He sounded like an idiot. Even in a text, his mom would know something was up. The woman always did.

The cab stopped in front of the Paris Hotel, leaving him without a choice but to hit send. There was no time to figure out a better way to lie because things were far from okay.

He slapped a wad of bills into the cabbie's hand and stepped out of the car. Beth emerged right behind him, still eerily silent. The lack of chatter spoke volumes about just how much he'd hurt her feelings. She tucked a strand of dark-brown hair behind her ear and sighed as she walked past him into the hotel. Her normal jaunty swagger had disappeared, thanks to him and his big mouth.

You're a real asshole, Layton.

She wasn't like Amanda. Hell, he doubted Satan himself was as bad as Amanda. But he'd lashed out at Beth as if she was his ex-wife incarnate. Why was he still letting that manipulative woman influence his actions? If he didn't figure out how to shake off her ghost, he may as well give up on winning Beth over. The rub was, he had no idea what to do now besides follow Beth into the hotel and make sure she was safely on her panel before he paid a visit to Little Elvis.

Nodding at the bellboy, he quickstepped into the hotel and spotted her glossy, dark hair moving through the throng of gamblers sitting in a trance at the one-armed bandits. She cleared the slot machines and took a right turn at the elevators. Hustling, he caught up with her in the walkway leading to the conference rooms. Nervous sweat made his hands clammy and he wiped them on his jeans before grabbing her wrist.

"Beth." No other words came. He had no idea what to say next, but he had to say something before it was too late.

She jerked to a stop, her face a dispassionate mask, mouth in a neutral position and her eyebrows arched. Her chin jutted forward as she tilted her face upward toward his. When her lips curved upward into an almost-smile, his stomach sank.

"You were right, Hank. I haven't been fair with you, so let me be now." She peeled his fingers one by one from her tiny wrist. "I'm your little sister's best friend, nothing more and nothing less. Let's just forget about what happened."

He stepped in front of her, blocking her path in a desperate attempt to salvage the tenuous connection they'd forged. "Look, I owe you—"

"No, you don't owe me anything." She glanced around him and gave someone in the crowd a little wave. "I need to get to my panel."

Looking behind him, he spotted Sarah Jane Hunihan marching toward them like Patton bearing down on the Germans in Italy. Judging by the snap, crackle, pop in her eyes visible at twenty paces, the normally sweet-natured old biddy was more than a little ticked off. But by the time she stopped in front of them, the angry spark had melted away as if it had never been there at all. But the spit-and-vinegar attitude seemed more natural somehow, an impression he filed away to consider later.

"There you are! We've been looking for you everywhere since you missed the morning sessions. I was so worried that something had happened to you." She clasped her hands together so tightly her knuckles turned white. "Goodness, this is such a dangerous city that I feared the worst."

Beth smiled down at the firm's executive secretary and the gaggle of attorneys behind her. "Nothing to worry about, Sarah Jane. I forgot to set my alarm, that's all."

"I expect more out of my best associate than that, young lady. Especially at a high-profile event like this." Ed Webster stood with his arms crossed, his mouth so tightly pursed it looked like he'd just sucked a pound of lemons. "If it had been anyone but you, they'd be on the next plane home Don't let this happen again."

"Now, Ed, that seems a bit extreme. I don't need to remind you that we've all made a few mistakes in our lives, do I?" Sarah Jane's indulgent smile didn't quite eliminate the venom thick in her tone. "Anyway, Beth is one of those lucky people who manage to land on their feet no matter what plans fate has made."

Webster shuffled a few steps back from Sarah Jane, bumping into Phil Harris, Mason Carter and Charles McMillian, who had been standing in his shadow, as usual. The firm's junior partners sidestepped out of Webster's way, mumbling their apologies and eyeing each other nervously.

A light sheen of sweat dampened Carter's forehead and he swiped at it with a handkerchief before taking a step away from the group. Harris drew a pack of cigarettes out of his pocket. He shook a single out and stuffed the pack back into his jacket.

"Nasty habit," Webster growled at Harris before striding down the hall toward the conference registration table, Carter and McMillian on his heels.

"Not to worry, you two." Sarah Jane looked between Beth and Harris, patting Beth's hand reassuringly. "He'll get over it. He always does. Now, Beth, let's get you ready for your panel presentation." The older woman linked her arm through Beth's and together they walked down the hall.

Hank couldn't look away from them. She would turn and give him a last look, then everything would be okay, he was sure of it.

Tension locked his muscles tight the farther away she got until his bum knee throbbed. They stopped in front of an open door and she laughed at something Sarah Jane said.

Now. This was when she'd give him a nod, a wink, a sign of some sort.

Instead, she shook her head and strode into the conference room, never glancing back.

Wasn't that a kick in the balls? All of a sudden his knee became the least of his aches and pains.

"Ms. Hunihan is right. He's all thunder without the lightning." Harris took a deep drag off the cigarette, closed his eyes and let the smoke out in a long exhale. The worry line between his eyes eased away and he brought the cigarette to his chapped lips again.

It took Hank a second to realize the junior partner was referring to Webster. "Uh-huh, is that why you're smoking like a condemned man?"

Harris chuckled and winked at him. "Yeah, well...when he just gets to know me a little better, understands who I am, it will all be different. I know it will."

Yeah, right. Webster was a first-rate asshole. Anyone with eyes could see that. "Good luck."

Stubbing out the cigarette in a freestanding ashtray, Harris nodded. "Thanks. I appreciate that." He took a few steps, then stopped. "And don't worry about Beth. I'll keep an eye on her."

His cop radar went nuts. Was Harris involved? He puffed up his chest and loomed over Harris. "What do you mean, 'keep an eye on her'?"

"Webster. To make sure he doesn't blow up at her." With that, he disappeared into a group of twenty or so attorneys milling around outside the conference rooms.

It made sense, but... Shit, he'd become so mixed up that even a chimney like Harris was starting to look suspicious.

Torn between standing guard like an unwanted mutt or tracking down the thugs from last night, Hank hesitated. His cop sense had all of the hairs on his forearm reaching for the sky. Everything looked normal. Everyone acted normal. Everything should feel normal, but it didn't. Something was off.

Listening to his gut, he marched toward the conference room. Through the open door, he saw Beth sitting behind a long table at the front of the room fiddling with some papers in front of her. A crowd of attorneys filed into the lecture hall through the other door to sit in the several hundred empty seats. Folks from her firm buzzed around the dais.

Fine. Everything was fine.

Damn, he couldn't afford to overreact to every twingy feeling. Nothing would happen to her in a room full of hundreds of people. Time to go make Elvis sing.

ഔഔഔ

The Little Elvis Wedding Chapel didn't look any better in the light of day. It looked a hell of a lot worse.

In a town full of tacky, this velvet-and-gold shrine to a man who'd died on his toilet stood in a class of its own. A six foot tall papier-mâché Elvis in a well-filled-out white jumpsuit with a suspicious eye stood next to a large hand-printed sign urging the marriage-inclined not to spill their drinks as they walked down the aisle.

While Hank waited for Little Elvis to finish a phone call in his office, he flipped through the velvet (of course) covered scrapbook on the reception counter. No matter what people may think of Elvis impersonators, this one was damn good at his job. The man was the spitting image of Elvis—a fat, short Elvis, sure, but Elvis all the same.

Someone coughed softly behind him. Hank glanced over his shoulder to find Little Elvis, dressed in jeans and a red-and-blue striped golf shirt but with his hair in the young Elvis pompadour, standing behind him.

"How may I help you, sir?" he asked in a clipped British accent.

Startled, it took Hank a minute to confirm the voice really did come from the man standing in the open doorway of the office. Who'da thought? Chalking it up to all the weird things life threw at you, Hank strode to Little Elvis and stuck out his hand.

"Thank you for seeing me. I'm Dry Creek County Sheriff Hank Layton and I'd like to ask you a few questions."

The man glanced at the extended hand, then crossed his arms over his chest. "And where exactly is Dry Creek County?"

Lowering his hand, Hank's best aw-shucks grin tightened. "Nebraska."

"You're out of your jurisdiction, Sheriff."

"Yeah, I get that a lot."

That earned him a quirked eyebrow. The man gave him a considering look and his small green eyes stayed locked on Hank's face. "You were here last night. I believe you barged in on the nuptials of a Georgia and Franklin Beauchamp."

"Yep, that was me alright, and that's why I need to ask you a favor."

"Mmm-hmmm. It's always good to have law enforcement owe you a favor, even if he's from as far away as... Nebraska, I believe you said?"

Hank nodded.

"Alright then, sheriff, I'm Alistair Armstrong. Please join me in my office where we can chat in peace."

Following Armstrong into the office, he stopped dead as soon as he crossed the threshold. The room was as understated as the lobby was garish. Cool blue paint covered the walls, punctuated with a crisp white trim. Large black-and-white candid photos of Elvis backstage preparing for concerts decorated the walls in the few spots where floor-to-ceiling bookshelves didn't take up all the space. The only available seat was a dark-blue wingback chair.

Armstrong walked behind a large oak desk, took a few steps upward and sat down on a full-size black chair. He must have noticed a quizzical look on Hank's face because a slight flush deepened the pink of his round cheeks.

"It's a step stool. The small things make life more convenient, don't you think, Sheriff?"

Hank settled into the wingback chair. "That I do."

"So, how can I assist you?"

"I'd like a copy of your surveillance video from last night."

"Really?" He steepled his fingers and tapped them on his chin. "What makes you think I videotape my customers?"

"The right eye of the craft-project Elvis in your lobby looks an awful lot like a camera lens."

Armstrong chuckled and leaned back in his seat. "Score one for the hick sheriff. Okay, I videotape my customers, for my own protection of course."

Thinking for a moment of the money that could be made by Las Vegas wedding chapels that sold photos of celebrities making very bad marital choices, Hank laughed. "Uh-huh. Wedding chapels must make excellent pickings for...burglars." He leaned forward, resting his elbows on his knees. "Whatever the reason you use the camera, I need to see the tape."

"Why?"

"Does it matter?"

"Yes, actually, it does. You see, this is my chapel and here, I am the king."

"No pun intended."

"Of course not. Now, why do you want it?"

Hank sat back. His seat sat lower than Armstrong's, allowing the two men's eyes to be at the same level. Neither's gaze wavered. Taking in the other man's placid, wrinkle-free forehead, Hank realized he had no power here. He couldn't demand the tape or threaten him with jail. Shit, he was lucky Armstrong was even talking to him. Gut churning, he did what no cop liked to do, he told a civilian about his case.

Except for a few raised eyebrows, Armstrong's face showed no reaction to Hank's tale. "So you're acting knight to the breathtaking senorita's damsel in distress? How very noble of you." He paused for a moment. "Why?"

The vein in Hank's temple began to throb. Like everything else that involved Beth, the process of gaining the video evidence wasn't going to be easy. "Because in Nebraska, that's how we're raised."

"Bollocks." He slapped his hand down on the desk. "Tell me the real reason."

Heat rushed up Hank's back and his muscles tensed. This was going all wrong. "What do you care?"

"I am passionate about two things in life: Elvis and love." He spread his arms wide to encompass the room. "The Elvis I have. The love, unfortunately, I do not. It's not my stature that seems as off-putting to the ladies of Las Vegas. Strangely enough, it's my devotion to Elvis Presley. Sadly, I will not give up one for the other. So, I satisfy my passion for romance by helping others achieve it. I saw the way you two kissed last night. There is no doubt in my mind that you two should be married, and I'd like to be the one to officiate at the event."

Armstrong's mouth kept moving but all Hank could hear was a loud buzzing, as if bees had dive bombed both ears.

Of course, he'd happily walk down that path again with Beth. Unfortunately, she had made her views perfectly clear this morning about moving from flirtation to a relationship. Still, his stomach vibrated and not with an about-to-lose-lunch way but with an at-the-top-of-the-roller-coaster-about-to-speed-down kind of excited anticipation.

"Sheriff, you've gone a bit green around the gills."

"She's my little sister's best friend. That's all."

"Mmm-hmmm. So then, there's no harm in giving me your word that the wedding will be here if you two were to ever get betrothed, since, of course, it will never happen?"

Sweat slicked the inside of Hank's palms. It was fourth down, time for the former big college quarterback to turn on his game face. Hank smiled, but made sure the grin didn't reach his eyes. "Sure, of course. How could I not share that moment with the man who was kind enough to share his surveillance tape?"

Armstrong's upper lip curled in a perfect copy of Elvis' rock-n-roll snarl. He tapped his fingers on the desk and gave Hank a considering look. His narrow shoulders shrugged and he pushed away from his desk before stepping down from his chair.

"Follow me, Sheriff." Little Elvis started humming, *I Can't Help Falling In Love With You,* as he strolled to one of the white bookshelves. A click sounded when he pushed one of the books forward and two shelves swung open to reveal a flat-screen TV, a tall stack of DVDs and a DVD player.

"I'll be damned," Hank muttered.

Armstrong pulled out the one on top of the pile and popped it into the DVD player. A menu appeared on the screen. Pointing a remote at the player, he clicked on Scene Selection and selected a black-and-white photo of Hank and Beth.

"The camera is connected to a motion sensor that detects when someone comes into the lobby. It whirs into action and records as long as the lobby is occupied. When there's no movement for five minutes, it turns off until the next time."

"You're full of surprises aren't you?"

Pride gleamed in Armstrong's eyes. "Yes, appearances can be deceiving."

They turned their attention to the screen. Hank came through the door first, followed by a weaving Beth. He watched himself scope out the lobby. When he saw Beth rub his cock through his pants, it was as if he could feel her long fingers wrapped around him and his dick twitched to life. Damn. This wasn't the place and definitely not the person he wanted to watch this with. He snatched the remote from Armstrong's stubby fingers and hit fast-forward, ignoring the man's chuckle.

He hit pause when the two thugs appeared on the screen. "You got zoom on this thing?"

Armstrong held out his small hand. "The remote, if you don't mind?"

Hank handed it over without looking away from the screen. The men's faces became larger on the TV. He searched for something familiar about the two men. Nothing. He'd never seen them before, but Beth may have.

"Can you burn me a copy?"

"I'm afraid that's not possible, Sheriff. There is other...information on this tape that needs to stay only with me."

Clenching his jaw, Hank tried to think past the frustration.

"However, I can print off a few screen shots."

"Armstrong, I could hug you right now."

"I'd prefer you didn't. Save that for your lovely lady on your wedding day, Sheriff."

Chapter Fifteen

Beth needed an IV coffee drip. STAT. Unfortunately, it had yet to be invented. Just as bad, Phil Harris blocked her from the silver coffee carafe on the snack table. The entire area surrounding the drink station was deserted, except for Phil. He ignored her please-move body language and kept his large frame parked in front of the coffee.

"So, what happened to you last night?" Phil leaned in, popping her personal bubble.

"Not much." Besides being drugged, followed by a couple of goons and waking up in a strange hotel room with Hank's fingers wrapped around her breast, not that one of the boss's minions needed to know that.

"Oh, I know the drill. What happens in Vegas, stays in Vegas."

Beth sighed. "I need a cup of coffee, Phil."

Instead of moving out of her way, he grabbed her elbow and wheeled her around toward the door. "You don't want this sludge. Come on, I'll buy you a cup and we can talk."

A chill brushed across the back of her neck. With all that had happened recently, there was no way she wanted to go have a private chat with Phil. "After the panel we just finished, I think I'm all talked out."

He tightened his grip on her elbow. "You must've seen the note by now. We need to talk."

The yellow note stuck inside her research file about Haverstan? Fear crawled across her skin like a platoon of army ants. "That was you?"

"Come on." He edged closer. "We'll talk about it outside."

His fingers dug into her bones, triggering her flight or fight response. "No way in hell am I going anywhere with you."

"Look, I'm trying to help you get out of this mess. It's gone too far." His gaze darted around the room. A light sheen of sweat appeared on his bald forehead. "I can't do it here, but come with me and I'll tell you everything."

No way should she go anywhere with Phil. Was he insane? Was *she* for even considering it? Because she couldn't deny the offer of the answers she desperately wanted was tempting. Anyway, it was Phil—dumpy, lumpy, chain-smoking Phil. If they talked somewhere public, he couldn't pull anything on her. Even if he did, she could knee him in the balls before he even blinked his eyes. Right?

"Please, Beth. I need to get this off my chest and you need to know what's going on." Sincerity poured from his gaze. So did fear.

"Why are you scared, Phil?"

"Not here." Like a trapped animal, he scanned the room as if looking for predators about to swoop down on him. He let go of her elbow, patted down his suit jacket, slid a hand into the left pocket and pulled out a pack of cigarettes. "Please." He tapped a cigarette out of the soft pack and slipped it back into his pocket.

Going with him was stupid. No doubt about it. But she couldn't *not* do it. Phil may be the weak link in the chains of secrecy wrapped tight around Haverstan. She hadn't found anything but dead-ends and corporate lies in her research and couldn't afford to miss an opportunity to uncover more. Last night proved events were spiraling out of control.

"Okay, but we're going somewhere with lots of people." Hank was going to kill her, but at least she'd text him. "Let me get my cell phone and briefcase. They're still on the dais."

Phil's face went white and he dropped his cigarette. "Sarah Jane's there." He tugged her toward the hall, leaving his cigarette on the floor. "She...she'll watch over them."

As she passed through the lecture room's door, Beth glanced over her shoulder and made eye contact with Sarah Jane. The older woman's penciled-in eyebrows were drawn together, disapproval radiating from her like a harsh wind that blew against Beth's skin and left her wondering what the hell was going on.

Ten minutes later she sat down at a bistro table tucked away into an alcove of a mock Parisian cafe on the other side of the casino from the convention area. The cafe was crowded with tourists grabbing a bite to eat between shopping expeditions and rounds of poker. Lucky for her, Phil couldn't light up in here. Unlucky for her, she'd had to stand with him outside the cafe while he'd sucked down two cigarettes, one right after the other.

The beefy estate attorney fiddled with his green plastic lighter and fidgeted in his seat. He'd loosened his blue-and-red striped tie as they'd rushed away from the lecture hall. Now it barely formed a knot, he'd tugged it so far away from his thick neck.

She'd been in enough staff meetings with Phil to know he wasn't one for comfortable silences. He was either freaked out, had no idea what to say or wanted her to be the first one to speak.

Too bad, Phil. You're out of luck today, you're going first.

Keeping her gaze locked on him, she brought the ceramic cup of coffee to her mouth. The heat touched her lips before the dark liquid. As soon as she swallowed, the warmth emanated outward, relaxing her tight shoulders.

"Alright, fine."

Hiding the smile behind her cup, Beth leaned back into her seat, hoping her nonchalant pose would hide her eagerness for Phil's story.

"So you know the casino that's getting built on the Lakota Reservation?"

She nodded. "Sure, it's big talk."

He leaned forward and lowered his voice. "Well, your land butts right up against the reservation. Tribal leaders have decided to build it right off of Highway 28, half a mile from your grandparents' front door."

"You're behind the times, Phil. They announced the casino would be off Highway 5." At least that was what she'd thought until this morning.

"It's a smokescreen so their partner can buy up the land on the other side of the reservation cheap."

"What makes you think this conspiracy theory is real?"

He dropped his gaze to his lighter. "I have my sources."

Phil was a junior partner, not a CIA operative. The guy didn't have sources, he had golf buddies.

"Look, I came here hoping to get some answers, not a bunch of speculation." She started to stand, but his hand shot out and grabbed hers.

"Do you really think someone would put out a ton of cash to buy land on supposition? On a guess? Hell no. The Haverstan Corporation bought the land cheap and is going to sell it to gas stations, strip malls and hotels for a big profit. We're talking tens of millions of dollars to be made here."

She sank to her chair with a thunk and tugged her hand out of Phil's grasp. "Go on."

"The Lakota planning committee is getting a cut of the profits from the land deal in exchange for announcing that the casino will be built off Highway Five. But their agreement came at a price. They didn't want a cut of just some of the land profits. They wanted a cut of *all* the land profits. Meaning everyone had to sell to Haverstan or the tribe would move the casino's location. Shit, they could cut a deal with another set of developers tomorrow, but they think they'll give a larger share of profits from this deal. Your grandparents' house is all that sits between Haverstan and a total monopoly."

"Shit."

"Damn straight. Now do you understand why you have to sell? Haverstan won't stop. They'll find a way."

Beth contemplated the dark abyss of her coffee, pushed past the anxiety and gathered her thoughts. Phil's story rang true, but he hadn't told her everything. "Who's behind Haverstan?"

He shrank back in his seat. "I can't tell you that."

"Why not? Have they threatened you too?"

"No. My cooperation came freely, but I don't like the nasty turn things have taken. She promised me no one would get hurt, but I heard you almost did last night."

She? "It's not too late, you can stop this. Bring it out into the open and you will."

Phil looked over her shoulder and his face went pale. "No. I've told you everything I can. You have to sell Beth, there's no other choice."

Glancing behind her, she spotted Sarah Jane walking through the cafe entrance.

Phil grabbed her hand, pulling her attention back around to him. "You have to sell."

A shiver ran down her spine. The fear in his eyes made her consider relenting. It was just a house. Her grandparents wouldn't have wanted her risking getting hurt to keep it. Selling was the easy thing to do. A no-brainer really. Except it wasn't her brain that stopped her from cashing in. Some indelible familial tie connected her to the little farmhouse where she'd been raised. Even if she never lived there again, it would always be her home.

"No."

He deflated in front of her like a child's party balloon and sank back into his seat. Defeat hanging heavy in his sunken eyes and deep worry lines carved into his prematurely bald head combined to make him seem much older than his twenty-eight years.

"So this is where you two snuck off to." Sarah Jane lowered herself into a spare chair and laid Beth's briefcase on the table. "I've been looking everywhere for you. I didn't want you to lose this."

"Thank you."

"Oh, you bet." She patted the yellow-and-blue plaid cloth tote bag at her feet. "I keep scrapbooking materials and my favorite stamps in mine. You never know when inspiration will strike."

Phil pushed away from the table and stood. "Ladies, if you'll excuse me, I'm going to go out in the hall for a smoke. I'll see you later."

"Darn, I was hoping you could help me carry a box from the business office to the convention hall." Sarah Jane paused for a moment. "But I'm sure you don't have time for that."

"I can help."

"Aren't you the sweetest, Beth, but it's a big box and really I need a man's help. Don't you two worry, I'm sure I can pay a bellboy to haul it for me."

A strained smile tugged at Phil's cheeks. "We can't have that. I'd be happy to help."

"Wonderful." She stood. "Let's be off. We'll see you later at the reception, Beth."

"Yes, ma'am."

Watching the two of them walk off, it struck Beth that she'd known Sarah Jane for most of her life, but the niggling feeling in her gut telling her she had missed something had grown into an ache.

She had to have turned into a paranoid mess to even imagine Sarah Jane as a criminal mastermind. She was a senior citizen scrapbooking fanatic, for God's sake.

She pulled out a legal pad and the Haverstan file from her briefcase, uncapped a black pen and drew a vertical line down the center of a page from the pad. In an organized fashion, she listed what she knew about Haverstan on one side of the paper. The list was regrettably short. On the other side, she wrote a much longer list of questions she still needed to answer, most notably, who was behind Haverstan and were they the ones who had drugged her last night. At that, her pen stilled. Until she got back home, there wasn't much she could do. Unless...

Digging her phone out of her briefcase, she ignored the unease swirling around in her stomach and punched in the number she'd first memorized in sixth grade. This would not be a comfortable conversation, but there were only a handful of people in Dry Creek, Nebraska, who knew where most, if not all, the bodies were buried.

"Layton residence."

"Hi, Mrs. Layton, it's Beth."

"So Hank tells me you're not my daughter-in-law," Hank's mother said without preamble. "What kind of foolishness have you two been up to? Imagine if the Junior Leaguers got ahold of this information. It would be all of town in an hour flat."

Yep. This was going as expected, but if she'd learned anything growing up as Claire's best friend, it was the best way to deal with Glenda Layton was to be blunt. "Nothing. It was just a mix-up. No wedding. No divorce. No nothing."

"Mmm-hmmm." Translation: You're full of it.

"Speaking of gossip—"

"Gossip? I've never gossiped a day in my life."

Beth shook her head. Glenda could easily operate a clandestine intelligence-gathering operation in her sleep. "You're right, I misspoke. I'm trying to get some information about a company called Haverstan, they've been buying up the land around my grandparents' place."

"Interesting. I haven't heard that name in forever and a day."

"You've heard of them?"

"Sure." Her strong voice turned wistful. "When I was growing up, there were Haverstans all over Dry Creek County. Cecil Haverstan, he was the cute one, died in Vietnam. Two of the cousins died of fever when we were in grammar school. Most everybody else scattered to the four winds in the seventies."

"So no one's left?" So much for old-school intel.

"Let me think...Cecil's cousin, Robert Reynolds, died a few years back, so that leaves only Sarah Jane Hunihan."

Beth straightened and glanced up at the door Sarah Jane had walked out of minutes ago. "What?"

"Oh yeah, she's a Haverstan on her grandmother's side. You'd never know it to look at her now, but that one was a hellion in her younger days. Had boys from six counties mooning after her, but she ignored them all. That girl had her eyes on a bigger prize than a bunch of cowhicks."

"What was that?"

"Oh, I never really paid attention to the talk. You know what Dry Creek is like now; imagine how bad the gossip was before reality TV and the Internet."

Beth waited, certain Glenda wouldn't be able to help herself from spilling the beans.

"Well, I can tell you this much. Sarah Jane had her eyes on moving into the big houses in the Big Horn Hills. She had a plan, I don't know what it was but that girl changed herself—from the shoes on her feet to her big blonde hair—into the spitting image of a country club wife, just without the husband. Then one day she chopped off her hair, bought the place near your grandparents and became the scrapbooking fiend she is today."

"What happened?"

"I have no earthly idea, but I think the question you need to answer is *who* happened. Not that I would know, because I don't gossip."

In a knee-jerk reaction to Glenda's proclamation, Beth rolled her eyes.

"Wow." Who would have ever thought? Could Sarah Jane be the one behind Haverstan, the threats and the drugging? Improbable didn't even begin to describe her level of doubt, but she couldn't shake a sinking feeling that the monster behind everything carried a plaid tote bag filled with stamps and scrapbooking pages.

"People your age never seem to realize that us old folks had lives before you came along, and continue to even after you're here."

Mind spinning, Beth took a sip of lukewarm coffee. "Well, thanks for the background, Mrs. Layton. I'd better go now—"

"Oh no you don't. I want to know what's going on with you and Hank."

Damn. Glenda wasn't about to let her get off easy. The problem was, Beth couldn't even explain to herself the two-steps-forward-and-three-steps-back relationship she had with Hank. "I wish I knew."

"Well, you'd better figure it out soon. That boy's been making a public spectacle of himself chasing after you. Don't think I haven't noticed." Her voice softened. "I love you like my own daughter, Beth, but you need to either take him up on his offer or put him out of his misery because I want some grandbabies before I'm too old to spoil them properly."

Grandbabies. The word socked her straight in the gut. Swallowing past the lump in her throat, Beth tried to stop the tears filling her eyes. "I'll do that, Mrs. Layton."

"You're the first girl to make him forget about Amanda and I'm hoping you'll make that permanent. But even if you don't, you're welcome at our Sunday dinner table anytime."

Touched by this acceptance, Beth blinked back tears. "Thanks, Mrs. Layton."

"And tell that son of mine to stop being a big fat chicken and call his mother."

Beth swept her notepad and pen into her briefcase and stood up so fast she knocked her chair to the ground. It clattered against the tile floor, turning everyone's attention her way. She smiled wanly, righted the chair and speed-walked out of the cafe. Discombobulated by the information floating around her head, she was certain of only one thing—she had to find Hank.

Swerving around a slow-moving couple in matching Las Vegas T-shirts, she headed toward the conference rooms. Hank had promised he'd be back for her after her panel. With any luck, he was hanging around, ticked off and wondering where in the hell she'd gone. When she told him that Sarah Jane Hunihan had rocketed to number one on the suspect list, he'd have to pick his jaw off the floor with a shovel.

The name Haverstan could be a coincidence, but she didn't think so. Still, she couldn't right the image of the scrapbooking woman she'd grown up next to with the land-hungry developer who had coerced families out of their homes and had sunk to vandalism and threats to get her to sell. Only two weeks ago she'd found Sarah Jane in the bathroom at work practically hyperventilating because of the stress brought on by the developers. A blast of cold air from a nearby vent brushed across the back of her neck, sending a shiver down her spine. Of course, what better way to hide your evil intentions than in plain sight?

Hurrying down the hall, she punched in Hank's number. No answer.

At the turn for the conference rooms, she spotted Sarah Jane and Phil going into the business center.

Fuck. If she went on to the conference room, she would lose them. Beth paused next to the information desk a few yards outside of the business center. She tried Hank again. Voice mail. She texted a quick call-me message.

Half hidden behind a sign for the national estate attorneys' conference, Beth watched the business center's open door, dreading and anticipating a Sarah Jane sighting. The coffee she'd just downed swirled around her stomach as her nerves sent her entire body on high alert. Half of her wanted to storm into the business office and demand the truth. The rest of her wanted to slink back to her hotel room and hide.

She'd eaten wild berry muffins with Sarah Jane at her kitchen table after her grandmother's funeral. Still hot from the oven, the muffins had been delicious and Sarah Jane had proved to be a sympathetic sounding board when Beth needed to talk out what she was going to do next with her grandparents' land.

Blinking, realization hit her. It had been Sarah Jane who'd brought the conversation around to her grandparents' house. Sarah Jane who'd first brought up the idea of selling. Sarah Jane who'd kept her up to date about all the other families who'd sold their property. Her knees weakened and the world tilted a bit on its axis.

It had been Sarah Jane who'd offered to complete the public records search of Haverstan. The company had hounded her, too, and she'd told Beth that even though she'd sold, she'd like to know more about them. And Beth had fallen for it, all of it, without a second thought. What an idiot she'd been.

Too antsy to wait a moment longer, she whipped around and plowed right into a wall of muscle and stumbled back. "I'm so sorry."

"All my fault. How about I buy you a drink to make up for being clumsy?"

The man's pale lips formed a smile, but it didn't reach his blue eyes. Everything about him was average, from his height to his bland brown hair, except for the one-inch scar on his chin.

Without meaning to retreat, she took another step back until the information desk counter bit into the small of her back. "Um, thanks but no."

His fingers clamped around her elbow like a vice. "Oh, come on now. Just a friendly drink."

This wasn't the first time she'd had to deal with pushy men at these conferences. They assumed that taking off their wedding rings would make women fall at their feet. Jerks. They were the morons who were the butt of every dishonest lawyer joke told since the dawn of time.

Accidentally on purpose, Beth stepped on the toe of his black shoe and leaned all of her weight into it. "I said no thank you."

The man laughed softly, but his smile disappeared. "I'm afraid you don't understand."

"Oh, I think I do. Your wife is at home, probably raising your two-point-five kids mainly on her own, while you jet off to conferences where you accost the waitresses and hit on every female attorney under fifty. Look. I'm not interested."

He took a step forward and something close to overwhelming panic skidded across her skin. She'd never seen him before but somehow he tripped the alarm bells in her head.

"So sorry to make you wait, ma'am. Is there something I can help you with?"

Beth turned her head at the no-nonsense tone of the hotel attendant at the information desk. The woman had addressed her, but was staring holes into the man.

Grateful for the backup, she smiled at the woman whose arms were crossed in front of her chest. Over the woman's right shoulder, she spotted two people who looked as if they hadn't showered in two days. She'd never been so glad to see them in her life.

"Sam! Chris!"

Claire's older brothers looked up and changed course, making it to her side in a few strides of their long legs. At the brother's approach, the stranger disappeared, melting into the crowd milling down the fake Parisian street, and she breathed a sigh of relief.

She sent the attendant a grin. "Actually, I found what I was looking for."

"Mmm, mmm, mmm." The woman shook her head. "I'd tell you to hit the tables, but it looks like you already hit the jackpot."

Glancing up at the Layton brothers towering over her, she tried to look at them with a fresh perspective. Even with the bags under his eyes, Chris couldn't hide the good humor in their Layton-family-hazel depths. Tall and good-looking with sandy brown hair and thick biceps, most women would be a little bit in love just at the sight of him. Her heart didn't even hiccup. As for Sam, well, he was the Adam Cartwright of the family—tall, dark and mostly silent. Serious as a heart attack, he leveled the same no-nonsense stare at her that sent his history students at Cather College scurrying.

Meeting his gaze, she sighed. He didn't do it for her either. Nope. Only Hank had ever made her stomach dive bomb to her toes.

"Everything okay?" Sam asked.

"Yeah, just an idiot who forgot he was married."

Chris held out his arm for her. "Come on. Let's go grab something to eat before I drop. I'm half dead from keeping up with Sam at the poker table last night."

"Little brother, I took it easy on you and you still couldn't keep up with me. You're just lucky that waitress nailed that guy in the head with her drink tray. Otherwise, you'd owe me even more of your millions in lottery winnings. Another couple of hours and you'd be in hock to me for some serious money."

"You wish." Pulling her hand through the crook of his arm, Chris headed toward one of the buffets.

Beth dug her heels in. "Sorry guys, but I can't join you. I have to find Hank. Have you seen him?"

Glancing back at the empty business center window, she wanted to stomp her foot. Sarah Jane must have left while she'd been distracted.

"Seen? No, but he called us from some Elvis place to keep you company until he got back. His cellphone had died and he couldn't remember your number. What's that about?" Chris asked.

Back? What was Hank up to? She checked her watch. She had two hours before the next conference panel about trust beneficiaries. Plenty of time. "It's a long story, I'll tell you at lunch."

"Good, and I'll tell you about how Sam couldn't tear his eyes away from the tattooed waitress long enough to figure out what cards he was holding. For such a boring stiff big brother, you sure do like 'em a little on the wild side. Who would've ever thought?"

True to form, Sam harrumphed and headed toward the buffet.

Chris didn't bother to keep his voice down. "It was an electric-blue dragon tattoo so big it barely fit on her upper arm. Hot. Very, very hot."

As they walked, a pair of yellow shoes in a shop window caught Beth's attention. Slowing her pace and looking closer, he gaze wandered over to the stranger's reflection in the window. He wasn't standing close to her but his cold and assessing image sent a shiver down her spine and she stopped dead in her tracks. He made a gun with his fingers and pointed directly at her.

Blood pounding in her ears, she spun around and searched for him in the crowd, but he'd disappeared as if he'd never been there.

Chapter Sixteen

*A*s the man on TV said, time to make it work. That was exactly what Sarah Jane had in mind.

Phil couldn't stop blubbering on as they rode the elevator to her room. She patted his hand absentmindedly while her mind whirled into action. Plan. She needed a plan. That bitch had convinced Phil to talk. He hadn't spilled everything, but enough that Sarah Jane had to accelerate things.

They got off on the twentieth floor, Phil still apologizing. Once inside her room, she couldn't take it anymore.

"Shut up and let me think."

He dropped into a desk chair and silenced his constant chatter.

The subtle approach hadn't worked last night. She wouldn't go that route again. The hired thugs, Stoliz and Daniels, could still be useful, however.

"Do you know where she's staying?"

"She's at the Bellagio."

"With the sheriff?"

"I don't think so."

Sarah Jane thought back to the way Hank had watched Beth this morning. Would he let her stay by herself after last night? Doubtful.

"Where is the sheriff staying?"

"I don't know."

"Then stop sitting there looking all sad and pathetic and find out."

His eyes widened.

Darn it, she didn't mean to be so harsh with him. "I'm sorry. I shouldn't have snapped at you like that. It's just we're so close to making everything perfect. It's only Beth standing in the way of us being a family together."

He sat up straighter in his seat and his face lost its confusion. "Give me five minutes." He grabbed his phone.

While Phil talked on the phone, she got her suitcase out of the closet and laid it on the bed. She tossed in the contents of the dresser drawers and closet. Next, she gathered her toiletries from the bathroom. It took less than five minutes to pack up her room.

"The Palms. Got it." Phil clicked off the phone. "What are you doing?"

"Getting ready to lead everyone on a wild goose chase while you work with Stoliz and Daniels to take care of Beth and the sheriff."

"What do you mean 'take care of'?"

She zipped shut her suitcase. "I mean kill them."

He jumped up from his chair. "Mother—"

She stopped him with a flip of her hand. She hadn't come this close to getting her revenge to be stopped by that bitch. She'd waited too long and risked too much. She had to make Phil understand.

"Your father favors her at work, do you like that?"

"You know I don't, but—"

"As Ed Webster's son, shouldn't it be you that he lavishes attention on?"

"Yes, but he doesn't believe I'm his son."

"He will. That's what I'm trying to explain to you. That's why we have to do this." She patted down his collar. "It's them or your family. Which do you care about more?"

ᔑᔑᔑᔑ

For the fiftieth time during the ten-minute cab ride, Hank stared at the closeup of the thugs from the Little Elvis Wedding Chapel. The smaller one had a narrow scar from where his chin must've been busted open. What he'd give to be able to give the asshole a few matching injuries.

He'd already e-mailed a copy of the photos to the Dry Creek Sheriff's Office. Chances were slim the men would pop up on a local search, but with luck, some of the national databases would reveal their identity.

The cab pulled into the taxi line at the Paris Hotel. Wallet at the ready, he pulled out a few bills and handed them over to the driver. "Keep the change."

The dry Las Vegas heat hit him as soon as he stepped out of the cab. Damn, he couldn't wait to get back to Dry Creek and the crisp fall weather. He'd had it with sweating his balls off in October. As soon as he walked into the casino, he scanned the crowd for Beth's brown hair even though he knew she'd still be in her panel.

But she wasn't.

He increased his speed as he made his way through the lines of slot machines surrounding the bar. She sat at the bar with her back to him, chatting with a guy in a dark suit. Damn it, he'd warned her to stay at her panel where there'd be lots of people she knew.

"Beth!"

She didn't turn.

The man whispered in her ear, giving Hank a perfect view of his profile. He turned, revealing a scar on his chin. The fucker was right here.

At the same moment, the man swept aside Beth's hair, revealing a stranger.

Where was Beth?

First relieved Beth hadn't been taken, Hank paused his march. But not for long. Fury at the perp who'd chased them last night blazed to the forefront. He popped his knuckles and stormed forward.

His target stood, oblivious to the world of hurt about to befall him.

Hank rushed up the three steps to the raised bar and shoved the goon away from the brunette.

Startled, the woman squeaked. Barstools scraped back as people scattered.

Surprise flashed in the man's pale blue eyes, quickly blotted out by recognition. The white scar on his chin stood out like a crooked bull's-eye.

The thundering feet of running security guards approached from behind.

In the half a second it took for him to pull back his fist, the man grabbed the brunette and flung her into Hank.

Thrown backward, he crashed back into the brass railing surrounding the bar. They both tumbled to the ground, the woman screaming at the top of her lungs.

One of the rotund security guards stopped next to them. The other two hoofed it after the perp sprinting out of the casino.

"What the fuck is your damage?" The security guard loomed over Hank, still flat on his back.

Hank assessed his options. From what the security guard observed, he'd just gotten his ass handed to him by a guy that he'd shoved. He didn't have any proof that Chin Scar was a danger.

The brunette stood and wavered on her feet. "Shooo shorry I fell into you."

"Ma'am, you didn't fall, he shoved you into me."

"Really? Wow." She plunked down onto her barstool and sucked on the skinny black straw sticking out of her old fashioned glass.

"Are you okay?"

She smiled up at him, her glassy eyes unable to focus. "Awesome."

It took him twenty minutes to convince the security team that he wasn't the bad guy. They'd made a copy of the photo of the two thugs he suspected of drugging Beth and escorted the brunette, who swore she'd only had two drinks, back to her room.

A quick phone call at the security office and he connected with Chris.

""Hey there big bro, how's it shaking?"

"Chris, tell me you're with Beth and she's okay." His lungs ached from holding his breath. Nothing in the world mattered as much as the answer.

"Well, she's stuck listening to a mini-lecture about the history of maps from Sam, so she's in danger of falling asleep, but other than that, everything's hunky-dory."

The news should have eased the flow of adrenaline through his veins, but it had the opposite effect. What if she hadn't been with his brothers? What if the asshole with the scar had found her and managed to drag her out of the hotel? He'd sure done a shitty job of keeping her safe.

"Where are you?"

"No need to get all growly. We're just leaving the buffet."

"Meet me at the front doors."

"Yes, sir."

Hank hung up without bothering to say goodbye. Anger rippled through him, mainly at himself for thinking Beth would be safe surrounded by a bunch of hungover lawyers at a convention. So concerned with making a score, he'd failed to protect the football. Rookie mistake. Well, it wouldn't happen again. He'd be damned before Beth left his line of sight.

Each minute seemed like hours as he waited, jumpy and nervous. He'd almost convinced himself that something had gone wrong, and then he saw her. Sandwiched between his haggard-looking brothers, her caramel skin glowing with a special light.

Hank felt it the moment their gazes met, all the way deep into the marrow of his bones, like the answer to a question he didn't know he'd asked.

His.

She sealed herself to his side. "We have to talk."

"Yes."

"Right now." They paused by the roulette table while Chris and Sam moved forward to watch craps.

"Spill."

"It's Sarah Jane."

That threw him for a loop. By the time she'd outlined what she'd learned from Glenda, her own experiences and from her chat with Phil, he was convinced.

"So what do we do now?"

"There is no 'we'. From now on, it's me. You're staying locked up in my hotel room with Chris and Sam until this is all over."

"Bullshit." She shoved a finger into his chest. "You wouldn't even know it was Sarah Jane if it wasn't for me."

"Doesn't matter. You're not in charge of this. I am. You can't control every aspect of everything. Why don't you just stop trying to?"

"Don't try to pull that crap with me, Hank Layton. It's my life. Not yours."

He couldn't shake the feeling that they weren't only arguing about Sarah Jane. Taking in Beth's flushed cheeks, the way her small tits heaved against that black dress and the desperation in her eyes, he surrendered. "Fine. Let's find out what room she's in."

Signaling to Chris and Sam to wait, he and Beth approached the hotel registration desk.

"How may I help you, sir?" The clerk stood at attention.

"We need Sarah Jane Hunihan's room number."

"I'm so sorry, sir, but we can't give out that information."

Hank flashed his badge. "Room number, please."

"Do you have a warrant?"

"No."

"Then no room number. However, I can call her if you'd like to see if she'd talk with you." The clerk hummed as her fingers flew across the keyboard. "Oh, it looks like Mrs. Hunihan is no longer staying with us. She checked out hours ago."

Chapter Seventeen

*T*rapped in the elevator at The Palms, speeding up to the fourteenth floor, Beth fought the urge to strangle Hank.

He'd gone all dark and surly the moment they found out Sarah Jane had checked out. A few phone calls later and his mood had gone from surly to irate. Sarah Jane had bought a last minute ticket to Mexico. The plane had been in the air an hour by the time they'd found out.

Tight, wound-up energy filled the elevator. It burrowed under her skin and plucked at her already high-strung nerves.

"Why are we going to your hotel room?"

Hank's heated gaze sent fire straight to her core. He only grunted in response.

Ass.

Mr. Grumpy needed to find someone else to take his bad mood out on because she'd find another room. It was a good plan but it left an aching need in the pit of her stomach and lower.

The elevator doors opened. Hank stepped out onto the floor and scanned the area, then held out his hand for her. Shooting him a dirty look, she ignored his hand and strutted down the hall to his room.

Hank opened the door and ushered her inside. "Wait here." Walking ahead, he looked into the bathroom and scoped out the rest of the room before making his way back to her. He closed the door and flipped the security lock.

Noting the empty bathroom and freshly made king-size bed, tension mounted inside her. "I don't know why you're so pissed off, but you'd better spit it out."

Instead of answering her, he crowded into her space, forcing her to back up until she was flat against the door. Her breath caught. Electricity sparked in the air around them, muddling her ability to form coherent thought.

"When I saw the guy from the chapel in the casino, I thought I was too late." Something dark swirled in the hazel depths of his eyes.

"Too late for what?"

"To save you. I thought I'd let you down." He lowered his lips to hers, possessive and hard.

Stunned, she couldn't move as his tongue teased her lips, sending heat flaring through her body. One thing she knew for sure in this twisted-up world was that Hank would never let her down. Ever. Need and want surged from her core. Forgetting the world and the dangers outside the door, she dropped her briefcase. The thunk it made when it hit the carpeted floor sounded a million miles away.

"Open your mouth, Beth."

Her nipples hardened at his growled command and, ignoring all the reasons why she shouldn't, she opened for him.

He deepened the kiss and his hands swept down her sides, coming to rest against the outside of her thighs. The silken lining of her black sheath dress felt so cool as it slid against her bare legs when he inched it higher and higher, until it bunched around her waist.

The contrasting texture of his rough hands and the delicate lace of her panties against her hip teased her desire. She buried her fingers in his thick hair, wanting to touch him everywhere at once. It was happening too fast and not fast enough. Lust overrode her need for control. She wanted what only he could give. God, she didn't think she could live another moment without it.

Desperate for more, she pulled back from his hungry mouth. "Hank."

He squeezed her hips. "No talking unless it's you telling me exactly how you want me to make you come."

Grabbing a handful of his button-up shirt in each fist, she looked him straight in the eye.

There was no going back.

Not for her. Not for him.

Not this time.

Buttons flew across the room when she yanked it open and exposed his muscular chest. His nipples hardened in the cool air conditioning.

"You want me to make you come?"

"Yes." The ache deep within her intensified. Her sensitive skin craved his touch, yearned for him.

"Say it."

Her mouth went dry, but his words had the opposite effect on her quickly dampening pussy. She didn't think she could say the words and give up that control. Then he leaned forward and nipped at the base of her neck. Her knees buckled and she would have sunk to the floor if his hands weren't holding her hips so firmly.

"I want you to make me come, hard."

His hands curved around to her ass, cupping each globe in his palms. "I don't know if you're ready for that. You seem more like a slow-and-soft kind of girl."

"I'm more than ready." She wound her arms around his neck.

He lifted her up to her tiptoes, his strong hands on her ass. Using a foot, he nudged her legs farther apart. The cool air brushed against her panties, taunting her heated clit.

"You want this?"

She shouldn't, not like this and not with him. Losing control with him would have fatal results for her heart, but her body overruled her head. "Yes."

"You want me to fuck you?"

His words vibrated against her neck. "Yes."

"Let go and I will."

"I..." Let go? She never let go.

Raising his head, Hank's gaze burned into her. "Just. Let. Yourself. Go."

And she did.

Shedding her iron self-control felt like peeling off a dress that was a size too small. All the pinching and constriction she'd grown used to and accepted as a fact of life disappeared. For the first time in years, she sucked in a full breath of freedom. There was no backup plan and no watching from a distance.

Her skin tingled everywhere Hank touched, but it wasn't him who'd made this happen. She had. The mixture of lust, power and joy opened her up to a whole new world of possibilities and hopes. Swearing to herself she'd never go back again, Beth closed her eyes and sealed the promise with a kiss.

Her lips busy with his, she spread her fingers wide and ran them across his broad shoulders. His woodsy cologne teased her as she continued her exploration. She followed the curve of his biceps, tensing under her touch, nudging his shirt down his arms until the dark material covered his long fingers and then fell from them.

Pulling her mouth away was a necessary small torture so she could taste more of him. His short beard tickled her lips as she trailed kisses down to his throat. She paused at the pulse hammering there, relishing that both of their hearts raced in anticipation. A quick nip elicited a harsh groan from him.

Pushing her back gently, he framed her face with his hands, forcing her to make eye contact.

"God, I've waited so long for you, Beth."

"I'm right here."

Something indefinable lurked in his eyes, a pain she eased the only way she knew how. Leaning forward, she kissed him again, teasing open his mouth with her tongue. For a moment he didn't move, then his hands seemed to be everywhere at once.

Hank disposed of her suit jacket in a quick move that would have made a stripper jealous. It dropped down beside her briefcase, followed a moment later by her dress and red-lace bra. She stepped out from the dress's confining circle, not wanting to be trapped anymore. His head dropped to her breasts and licked a line of fire across their top curves. Using his hands to mold the small orbs, he pushed them upward and sucked one dark-brown nipple into his hot mouth.

The moment his teeth grazed the hard nubs, Beth's legs gave out on her and she collapsed against the hotel door. Tension built inside her as his hand snaked down her flat belly. His hungry mouth released her breast and traveled back up to her mouth.

One hand slid lower, snuck under the elastic of her lace panties and a single finger sank between her wet lips. Her back arched in reaction to his touch, so pleasurable it nearly broke her. Eyes clenched shut, ribbons of color danced across her mind's eye, their hues becoming more vibrant as he stroked her clit and dipped first one, then two, then three fingers inside her sensitive pussy.

Trying to anchor herself to reality, she reached for him. Her fingers dug into his shoulders, but instead of bringing her back to the real world, the feel of his skin increased her need. It pushed her forward and brightened the colors behind her eyelids until they were nearly neon in intensity. The vibration built deep inside her, ratcheting up with each stroke of his fingers in and out. The corner of the hard, plastic fire escape sign on the hotel door dug into her shoulder blade, but urgent need nearly blinded her to any sensation but his touch. His fingers twisted within her slick folds, pushing her closer to release until the colors exploded and her orgasm overtook her.

Panting, Beth rested her head against his shoulder. She should be sated, but instead a fresh energy buzzed through her and she hungered for more of Hank inside her than just his fingers.

"Fuck me, Hank."

"Anything you want."

After how fast he got rid of her clothes, she wasn't surprised to see him divest himself of his pants in the blink of an eye. Then his lips captured hers and all rational thought fled, replaced by want and need.

Chapter Eighteen

Sliding his rock-hard cock inside her wetness, Hank drove deep into her pussy. She embraced his dick, massaging it with every stroke, and within moments he was on the edge of coming. Long, lean legs wrapped around his waist and her round ass filled his hands as he urged her body to slow down so they could make it last. The tips of her mocha-colored nipples rubbed against his chest. Her luscious lips on his throat made him want to forget his attempts to draw out the pleasure.

Her heels dug into the small of his back as she arched back, grinding her pussy against his cock. Fuck. If she kept that up, there was no way he would last another five minutes.

"Slow down, baby. I want to enjoy you."

"I thought you were." Her movements slowed but didn't stop and she swerved her hips in one direction then the other in a carnal figure eight.

"Oh God, Beth, not for much longer if you keep doing that."

Her unguarded laughter, so sweet and sexy at the same time, nearly sent him over the edge. He'd thought he had it bad for her before, when he didn't know what he was missing. Now that he did, there was no way he'd let her go. Shit, he was a fool for taking so long to realize it.

Hating himself, but knowing he had to do it, he withdrew. He grasped her narrow waist and pushed her against the door. Damn, she was beautiful. Her brown hair, going in all directions, brushed against her shoulders, hiding her long and delicate neck.

"Hank?"

"Shhhhh." He slid his hands up from her waist, inching them across her warm brown skin and up to her tits. High and round, they filled his palms as if his hands were made for holding them. "Let me touch you."

Rolling her nipples between his fingers elicited a low moan from her parted lips. Encouraged, he tugged them gently and dipped his head down to circle one nipple with his tongue before sucking it into his mouth. He'd never heard sweeter music than her groan.

Wanting to touch her everywhere at once, he forced himself away from her nipples. His tongue glided downward, stopping an inch higher than the start of her trim bush. She shivered under his hands when he kissed her there, his hands skimming across her hips, pulling her lower body closer to his needy mouth.

Bringing his thumbs to her wet lips, he spread them wide, exposing her clit. He flicked it with his tongue, tasting her, memorizing the moment. Using his last vestige of patience, he savored her essence, not wanting this to end but knowing he wouldn't make it much longer before he had to bury himself within her welcoming pussy once more.

As if she understood his quandary, Beth pushed his head away. "Fuck me now, Hank. I need to feel you inside me."

He wanted nothing more, but they couldn't. "I don't have a condom."

A shadow appeared in the depths of her eyes for a moment, before she blinked it away. "You don't have to worry."

"You're on the Pill?"

She blinked again. "No need to worry about babies with me." She claimed his mouth, her tongue wanting entrance and her body demanding so much more.

He picked her up, raising her high enough to straddle him. Flipping around so it was his back against the door, he leaned against the wood. Hands gripping her hips, he moved her up and down on his standing cock. So good. She felt so good against him and around him.

Beth braced herself on his shoulders and undulated. He couldn't wait; he already had played on the edge for too long. Already his balls were tight, ready to spill.

The slap of their bodies meeting filled his ears and a musky scent surrounded them. Her body, so warm and smooth underneath his palms, pushed him to go faster but he wanted to draw it out a little bit longer, just a little bit longer. He could make it last. Hold her longer. Bring her closer. Make her his. But then her body stiffened and her wetness squeezed his cock as she came. Her orgasm milked his cock and he gave in.

As they stood, bodies locked together, Hank realized he'd never felt so alive. Damn. Maybe a trip to the Little Elvis Wedding Chapel wasn't out of the question.

He searched his mind for doubts and found none. This was right. He'd known it for years. Now he just had to convince her.

"Beth... Honey, you and me, we fit. You've got to see it now."

She stiffened in his arms, but not in ecstasy this time. Something was different in how she held herself as she lowered her feet to the ground and stepped away from him. There was no mistaking the guarded look behind her thick eyelashes.

His stomach knotted.

"Where do you see yourself in five years?"

Her carefully worded question, delivered so softly, threw him. Was it the job? Not every woman wanted to be with a man in law enforcement. "Are you asking about the job?"

Her thick hair waved around her as she shook her head. "Personally."

He hesitated. He didn't understand why, but he could tell a lot rode on his answer. Maybe everything.

Swallowing, he tried to get his tongue to stop sticking to the roof of his mouth. If he'd had any idea what she wanted to hear, he would have blurted it out in a heartbeat. But he didn't, which left him with the truth. Pulling her into his arms, he stroked her hair.

"Us, together. Happy. A small house on a plot of land." The picture formed in his head so quickly, he must have been dreaming of it subconsciously for years. "A grove of trees as a windbreak around the house, one with a treehouse and a tire swing. Lots of open space for our kids to run."

Her shoulders convulsed against him. Hell, it must be the job.

"I promise, I'll be home every night. It's Dry Creek. It's not like we've got a huge crime rate."

She twisted out of his grasp, her head lowered.

"Beth, what is it?"

When she brought her teary gaze up to his, he held his breath, steadying himself as if for a physical blow.

"I can't give you that."

"What do you mean?"

She laughed, the sound harsh and torn. "This is the ultimate case of not being able to have your cake and eat it too."

"Beth..." His voice cracked, a poor imitation of the damage being done to his heart. She didn't move, didn't say a word, and Hank's chest hurt as if it were splitting down the middle.

Then, her brown eyes softened around the edges.

His shoulders relaxed and his heart rate came back to normal. "So we'll work through this, whatever it is."

Sighing, a look of forlorn kindness on her face, she brushed his hair back from his forehead and brushed his cheek with a kiss. "No, we won't."

Her hand slid from his and she slipped into her dress.

Before he could utter a word, the door thumped against his back. He ignored it, but the knock came again.

"Uh, Beth, are you in there? It's me, Phil." His words were muffled by the closed door, but the underlying desperation came through loud and clear.

In an instant, Hank was on full alert. What the hell? How had he found her here and why was he following her?

Beth slid her arms into her suit jacket. "What do you want, Phil?"

"It's about what we talked about at the coffee shop. You're right, I need to come clean, but please don't make me yell it through the door."

An itchy sensation danced down his spine, but he looked through the peephole and shucked on his pants. The fisheye view of Phil Harris showed him sweating and shifting his weight from foot to foot. Good so far, but still Hank couldn't shake the unease. Leaving the security lock on, he inched open the door. Damn, he'd be a shitload more comfortable if he hadn't had to leave his gun in Dry Creek. Eyeballing Harris through the slit, his body tensed, waiting for an unseen attacker.

"Come on, man, it's just me and I really need to talk to Beth."

"You alone?"

Harris' gaze never left his. "Yes."

Hank closed the door, flipped the security lock and opened the it. Harris stood by himself. The man's right eye twitched and he gulped.

He opened his mouth to speak, but before a single sound emerged, a soft pop sounded and the right side of his head exploded outward.

Blood splattered against the white doorframe.

Crimson rivers ran down the wood and puddled on the brown carpet.

Harris fell backward into the hall with a thump. Beth screamed.

Reflexively, Hank grabbed the door to slam it shut but a size twelve shiny, brown dress shoe blocked the move. Looking upward, he took in the black suit pants with sharp creases, two empty hands, the crisp white shirt decorated with a discreet navy-blue tie and, finally, to the ice-cold blue eyes of the thug from the casino.

The man smiled, revealing a large gap between his two front teeth. "I was hoping to run into you again."

Just like it had when he'd taken the field before a big game, the rest of the world disappeared. Hank focused all of his mind and energy on the snide little fucker who wanted to hurt Beth. Where was the gun? The man's hands were free at his sides.

At least a head shorter than him, the man had only one advantage, his foot in the door. Hank wasn't worried.

"You and me both, asshole." He slammed the door against the man's foot, holding it tight so he couldn't pull his trapped foot free. "Beth, get in the bathroom and lock the door."

She made a squawk of protest. He snuck a glance over his shoulder. She stood in a kickboxing stance. God save him from stubborn women. "This isn't your kick bag."

The thug had put all of his body weight into pushing the door open enough to almost squeeze out his foot. Locking his legs, Hank leaned into the door, looking through the peep hole right in time to see the asshole pull the gun from his shoulder holster. Another soft pop sounded and a mirror behind Hank shattered. That explained the location of the gun.

"Now, Beth!"

She hustled into the bathroom.

In the same breath, Hank released the room door and stepped backward toward the bed, his body as far away from the bathroom as possible in the tight space. He wanted the asshole focused solely on him.

Thrown off balance by the sudden release of pressure, the gunman stumbled into the room. He recovered his balance in two large steps and rushed forward with his gun hand leading. Just what Hank wanted.

Sweeping his right hand up and across, he connected with the attacker's gun arm. The momentum twisted the gunman's body and forced the Glock to point toward the floor.

Swinging his body around, he followed the attacker's awkward spin. With his left hand, he shoved the man's head down while at the same time wrenching the gun away and tossing it onto the bed.

Helping gravity along, Hank shoved the asshole to the floor. Digging his knee into the man's upper back, he yanked the perp's arm behind him in a grip guaranteed to hurt like hell.

The whole thing took about thirty seconds. Obviously, this guy was not a professional.

Amping up the pressure on the man's arm, Hank wanted to keep going. Another twist or two and the arm would snap like a twig. After what the bastard had put Beth through, nothing would be more satisfying. The idea tempted him beyond reason.

Bloodlust ran high as he turned the thought over in his head. His fingers tightened on the man's arm, ready and eager to do it. But he couldn't. No matter how good it would feel, he couldn't betray his ethics that way. He'd taken an oath he wouldn't break.

But this asshole didn't know that.

"What do you want?"

"Fuck off, you—" A quick twist turned the man's curse into a squeal.

He relaxed his grip. A little. "I'll only ask this one last time. What do you want?" In a dark place deep within, he hoped the gunman wouldn't answer.

"We were just going to grab her, scare her, but..." He dropped his head and mumbled into the carpet.

Grabbing a fist full of greasy black hair, Hank tugged. "But what?"

"The old lady changed her mind."

Sarah Jane. "What did she want?"

"She wanted her dead."

Hank's insides knotted. He glanced back at the closed bathroom door. A world without Beth? He couldn't imagine it. After today, he didn't even want to think about a day without her. Old lady or not, Sarah Jane was about to go down.

"What's her name?"

"I don't know."

"Bullshit."

"She never gave her name. I never even saw her. Only him."

"Phil?"

"Who?" The perp sounded truly baffled.

"The guy whose brains are all over the hall carpet."

"He brought the cash."

"So why kill him?"

"Didn't mean to. The gun, it accidentally went off."

An idiot with a firearm usually had that result. "Where's your partner?"

"What partner?"

"Really? Do we have to do this the hard way?" He twisted the suspect's arm.

"Okay, okay!" He let out a small puff of air when Hank loosened his grip. "He got pinched last night. DUI."

"You two sound like quite the pair."

A ruckus sounded behind him. Before he could jerk his head around, a deep, booming voice echoed through the room. "Hands up!"

Two uniforms stood in the doorway, guns drawn and in a firing stance. Shit. He could read their nervous thoughts from across the room. Calm. He had to bring the situation down before he ended up with a bullet.

"I'm Sheriff Hank Layton from Dry Creek, Nebraska," he said in the same tone he used with skittish animals. "I've apprehended a suspect who broke into my hotel room."

"I said, hands up!"

He did not want to let go, but there wasn't much of a way around it. Putting his full weight into the knee grinding into the goon's spinal cord, he unwrapped one finger at a time from around the man's arm and held his breath.

The asshole didn't move a muscle beyond letting his arm fall to the ground like dead weight.

Okay, this might work out. More confident, Hank raised his arms. "I have identification in my wallet. I'm going to reach around—"

He didn't get any further before the bathroom door flew open and Beth rushed out with a war cry.

Cop number one pivoted and fired in the same motion.

The room went silent except for the thump of Beth's body hitting the floor and a half second later, the sickening thud of what must have been her head bouncing off the tile.

"You fucking idiot! You just shot the victim!" Fear spiked so fast, bile rose in Hank's throat.

Taking advantage of the moment, the suspect jumped up and sprinted toward the door.

Hank didn't have time to process what had happened. Bounding up, he barreled toward the suspect, acting only on instinct and adrenaline.

Faced with a wall of blue in front of the open bathroom door, the man hesitated a foot outside of the uniformed officers' reach.

Just the opportunity Hank needed. He wrapped his arms around the man, taking him down hard, grinding his face into the carpet's brown fibers. "God dammit, put some fucking cuffs on him."

One of the officers hurried forward and clamped the metal closed around the suspect's wrists. The officer who fired stood in the doorway, a deer-in-the-headlights look in his dark eyes.

Blood rushed so loudly in Hank's ear, he almost missed hearing his name. It came like a soft breeze from the recesses of the bathroom and sent chills down his spine. Not bothering to get up, he crossed the three feet to the doorway on his hands and knees.

She lay so still, he couldn't stop thinking the worst had happened. "Beth?"

Her quiet moan sounded like a roar in the unnatural quiet around them.

"Darlin', I'm right here." He stroked her soft hair, continuing down to her shoulder, hoping to comfort her, but when he brought up his hand, a warm liquid covered it. Blood. Panic grabbed him by the throat. "Call an ambulance," he screamed, fear tight in his voice.

"It's on the way," the officer said.

Beth lay on her back, her thick, dark hair like a curtain across her face. Brushing it back, he sought the source of the blood. Though her eyes were closed and her face contorted with pain, he couldn't find a scratch. Drawing his gaze downward, he spotted the quickly widening circle of blood seeping through her suit jacket sleeve.

He grabbed a fluffy white towel from a shelf and pressed it against her right arm to staunch the blood flow.

She yelped and her eyes popped open, agony and confusion clear in their dark-brown depths.

"Help's coming. You got shot in the arm. I know it hurts like hell, but you'll be okay." God, he hoped so. He needed to say the words almost as much as she needed to hear them.

Chapter Nineteen

*B*eth grazed her fingers over the goose egg on the back of her head. Testing, she pushed. A sharp pain made her gasp for breath. If she'd been a cartoon character, that's when colored stars would have started circling her head.

"I always wondered if you pushed hard enough on a knot like that, if the swelling would pop out somewhere else." Chris Layton's head poked through the olive-green curtains surrounding her bed in the emergency room. He had a goofy grin, but serious eyes. "Just wait until I tell Hank I saw you without your shirt. His head will explode."

Automatically, her hands went to her chest, pressing the thin gown to her skin. At least it tied in the back. The EMTs had cut off her dress and bra right there in front of God and everyone in the bathroom. Not her best moment. What a weird thing to be concerned with considering, she'd just been shot. Must be the medicine they'd given her for the pain.

"Chris, you're a tease." Kidding him helped to cover her disappointment at it being Chris and not Hank. At least she hoped it did.

He wiggled his eyebrows. "I know, Mom says it's all part of my charm."

Someone she couldn't see cleared his throat behind the curtain. Chris rolled his eyes in an exaggerated motion and swung open the curtain to reveal Hank's other brother, Sam.

Behind them, nurses, doctors and orderlies buzzed around the busy emergency room. Beeps and squeaks from gurneys punctuated the constant murmur of people talking in hushed tones. The whole scene looked like something from TV, except when she watched *Hospital 911* in her living room, she couldn't smell the antiseptic.

"Pardon my idiot brother, the home training didn't take." Sam held out a white plastic bag from a drugstore. "I understand you, um, lost your dress. I picked up something for you to wear. Hope they fit."

Tears pricked her eyes. Even though she was just their little sister's best friend, the Laytons had always watched out for her. "Thank you."

"It's nothing great. Just a tacky hoodie and sweat-pant shorts."

"I wanted to get the hot-pink shirt that said 'topless showgirl in training', but Mr. No Sense of Humor vetoed it."

Sam's jaw tightened. The two had been like this for as long as she could remember. Probably since birth.

"Thank you for that, Sam." She didn't want to even imagine having to wear that on the plane ride home.

"The doctors released you?"

"Yeah, I'm free to go."

Chris stepped farther into her curtained-off area and peered at her head. "Wow, that is some bump. How's the arm?"

"The doctor said it went straight through, he just had to stitch me up. No sling or anything." Just talking about her gunshot wound made it throb.

"What were you thinking?" Chris asked. "If I didn't know any better, I'd think you were Claire, going off all full-on banshee like that."

Chris put his question out there bluntly, but it wasn't as though the thought hadn't gone through her head a million times since she'd opened her eyes to find Hank's worried face inches from hers. A few months ago, a killer had targeted Claire, and when he set her Jeep on fire, she'd chased him down like a woman possessed—and that wasn't the worst of it. She and Claire had been best friends forever, but Beth was the reserved one. Attacking someone was not her style.

It turned out gunshot wounds weren't all that unusual in Las Vegas, so she'd had plenty of time to ponder after the triage nurse declared her several rungs down the priority ladder.

The fact was she hadn't thought first. She'd been huddled in the bathroom, hearing all sorts of grunts, bangs and harsh words. Everything had quieted, but when she heard a new voice, she'd known Hank was outnumbered. Her Hank. She couldn't leave him to face that on his own; as long as there was breath in her body, she'd fight for him.

So she'd flung open the door and got herself shot.

Not that she'd tell Hank's brothers that.

"It seemed like a good idea at the time."

"You hang out with Claire too much if you've started thinking like that." Sam delivered the line dryly, but the undertone of love for his sister couldn't be missed.

That was the Laytons for you. Always in each other's business and giving each other a hard time, but she couldn't imagine their family working any other way.

Family. The word made her gut twitch. She'd always known how important having his own family was to Hank, but having him confirm it solidified her decision to keep her distance.

"So, where's Hank?"

"Still at the police department." Sam shrugged his shoulders. "Did you talk to the cops?"

"Yeah." Her mouth dried at the memory. She'd told the investigators about the threats, being drugged and everything else that had led up to today. When she'd told them her suspicions about Sarah Jane, she couldn't get over how surreal the whole thing was. From scrapbooking to murder-for-hire? It didn't seem real.

"What did they say?" Chris asked.

"That the guy who busted into Hank's room had confessed, but he swore he didn't know the name of the person behind it all. The detective confirmed Sarah Jane had checked out of the hotel, bought a ticket to Mexico and, hopefully, is gone forever." She couldn't stop herself from shivering.

Sam closed the gap between them and stiffly patted her on the shoulder. "I still can't believe that part."

"You and me both."

"Well, at least we know she's not here. Consider me your beefy and handsome bodyguard. Sam can tag along too." Chris looked down at the release papers on the bed. "Let's get out of here."

"Sounds good."

"I'm sure you'll feel better when you get home." Sam dropped the plastic bag onto the bed and grabbed Chris' arm. "We'll give you some privacy to change."

Both men walked out of the curtained area.

Beth's arm burned. When she squeezed her eyes shut, she pictured the spray-painted walls of her grandparents' trashed house.

The detective told her not to worry, but she knew Sarah Jane was out there. Waiting.

Pushing those thoughts aside, she threw off the covers and changed. Time to do what she always did. Move forward.

�������

Beth slid across the red vinyl booth seat at The Lucky Seven Diner. She fiddled with the dice-shaped salt and pepper shakers while Sam and Chris studied the menu as if it were the Holy Grail. Still nauseous from the pain medication, she had no intention of topping off the day by puking at the table.

"So, what'll you have?"

Hypnotized by the nutty scent of coffee wafting from the waitress' silver carafe, Beth almost missed the flush that turned Sam's cheeks ruddy. Flabbergasted, she didn't even pretend not to stare. Not that he noticed. A parade of showgirls wearing pasties and feathers could have danced by and he wouldn't have blinked. Looking beyond the coffee in the waitress' grasp, Beth studied the woman who'd captured Claire's buttoned-up brother's attention.

Wow.

The woman had a good two inches on Beth, making her about five feet, eleven inches tall in black high-top tennis shoes. Bright platinum-blonde hair fell in layers of riotous curls to her pointy chin. A tattoo in a rainbow of colors peeked out from the short sleeve of her black T-shirt, but not enough for Beth to determine if it was an animal or an intricate design. A pair of painted-on jeans and cherry-red lipstick completed the look. The waitress looked as shell shocked as Sam.

"Hey! I know you." Chris broke the silence. "You were one of the waitresses at our poker game. That jerk sure did deserve it."

"Uh, thanks." Her husky voice acknowledged Chris but her gray eyes never left Sam.

Chris put his elbows on the table and leaned around Sam to get closer to Beth. "It was awesome. This asshole..." He glanced up at the waitress. "Sorry about that. This jerk grabbed her tits..." He smiled an apology toward the other woman. "Sorry. This jerk grabs her...breasts during the poker game. So, she takes this ginormous silver tray that she'd been using to carry the drinks and whacks him over the head with it. It was a sight to behold."

He relaxed back, a goofy grin on his face. For his part, Sam had gone perfectly still. Interesting. She couldn't wait to tell Claire about her brother's very atypical behavior.

Beth flipped up her heavy ceramic mug. "May I have some?"

The waitress—Josie, according to her name tag—blinked a few times as if trying to remember why she was here. "Uh, yeah."

"Josie." Sam's low voice rumbled.

A tight smile pinched Josie's cheeks tight and her eyes darkened to the color of hardened steel. With a jut of her hip, the straightening of her spine and the tilt of her jaw, her body morphed from that of a friendly waitress to a hard-ass chick who just might steal someone's lunch money. "Do I know you?" She cocked her head to one side sending her curls bouncing. "Oh yeah, you were at the poker game too, right? Scotch, neat, if I remember correctly."

"I—"

"You're hungry? Well, you came to the right place. Let me get your orders." Holding her pen at the ready, she turned toward Chris. "What can I get you?"

After writing down the brothers' orders, Josie hurried back to the counter. There, she whispered with another waitress before disappearing into the kitchen.

"What in the hell was that all about?" Chris prodded.

"None of your business." Sam snapped his menu closed and shoved it into the menu holder in the middle of the circular table.

"Oh really, well—"

"Drop it."

Chris held up his hands in surrender. "Fine, whatever you say big brother... So you don't mind if I try to get her number?"

Sam's shoulders tensed and he got right into his brother's face until their noses nearly touched. "I don't care what you do. Go for it."

"Hey there folks, here are your drinks, two waters and a Coke." A middle-aged waitress with mousy brown hair carefully placed the glasses on the Formica table. "Josie went on break, so I'll be taking care of you from now on. Your orders will be right up." With a curt nod, she strode off.

Fixing Chris with a glare, Sam gulped down half of his water before slamming it down. "Don't say a word, Chris, not one single word."

Chris opened his mouth then, thinking better of it, clamped it shut.

Brothers. If they didn't love each other so much, they'd have killed each other long ago.

A bell jingled when the front door swung wide. Hank sauntered in, worry lines visible from across the room. But as soon as his gaze met hers, those lines eased and his lips curled into a relieved smile. Her heart flipped and flopped in her chest. If she didn't get a handle on her feelings, she was doomed.

"Hey." He sat down and stroked a wide palm down her hair, stopping at her shoulder. His hand rested there and her nerves buzzed with awareness. "Are you okay?"

No. Not as long as he touched her. Hell, not as long as he was in the same hemisphere.

"Fine, thanks for asking." She raised her injured arm, making it throb enough to distract her from Hank's touch, burning her like a branding. "A few stitches and I'm as good as new."

His hand slid up the column of her throat until he cupped her chin, tilting it upward. Her breath hitched and blood rushed in her ears, drowning out the clatter of silverware and shouts of "order up". Of its own volition, her body arched forward and her lips parted. A taste. She only needed a taste of him and she'd walk away.

The kiss scattered all thoughts of leaving. Her lips widened, welcoming his demanding tongue, and her own curled around it. A tingling started in the pit of her stomach and grew until she was on fire with wanting. Nipples hard and pussy wet, nothing else mattered but this moment, this kiss.

Hank could have tossed her onto the table and fucked her senseless while the short-order cook flipped hamburgers in the background. She wouldn't have given a damn.

"Okay then, I guess Sam and I will be taking our drinks over to the counter." Chris coughed, a noise that sounded suspiciously like laughter.

Dazed, Beth pulled away from Hank and licked her kiss-swollen lips. She should be embarrassed, but after all that had happened, she just didn't have the energy for it. Instead a languid sense of wellbeing had seeped into the marrow of her bones. A girl could get used to this.

She sighed, half in defeat and half in contentment. If she didn't put a stop to it, she'd get so used to it that she'd wake up one day knowing she'd stolen Hank's dream of having his own family of Laytons. Because there was no denying it, he wanted her just as much as she needed him. For both of their sakes, she had to get back to neutral territory.

"Ignore Chris, he's an idiot." Hank didn't even bother to glance over his shoulders at his retreating brothers. He scooted over, so close their legs touched from hip to knee.

His nearness was doing a number on her resolve so she moved sideways. Her gaze followed his as it took in the two-inch gap between them, then slid back up.

Desperate for something to fill the silence and break the sexual tension, she grabbed her coffee cup and inhaled its wonderful aroma. "So, what did the police say?"

His smile indicated he knew exactly what she was up to, but he didn't call her on it. She released a breath and her shoulders relaxed.

"That two-bit goon had Sarah Jane's e-mail address and cellphone number programmed into his phone. That plus the information you got from Phil and what you'd dug up on Haverstan on your own creates a strong case against her."

"But why?"

"Hell, I wish I knew. The mint to be made from owning the land around the road leading to the Lakota Reservation casino provides a great motive, but it just doesn't ring true. There's more to this than money. Once I track her down, I'll find out exactly what that is."

"So you're sure she's gone?"

"Yeah, there's a record of her checking into the flight to Mexico."

Apprehension inched across her skin and she couldn't stop the shiver of fear. "So what now?"

He curled his fingers around hers still holding the mug. "We go home. I'll find Sarah Jane. I'll do whatever it takes to keep you safe."

"Why?" Excitement and dread swirled around inside her, tensing every muscle in her body.

He chuckled. "Well, we can't live in Vegas."

The lump in her throat grew to boulder proportions, but she had to know. "That's not what I mean."

"I know." He shifted in his seat to fully face her.

She drank in the sight of him. The scruffy beard covering his strong jaw. The way the flecks of green in his hazel eyes grew darker as his mood turned serious. How his gray shirt did a lousy job of hiding the breadth of his muscular chest and curve of his well-formed biceps. Needing to memorize the moment before it all went to hell, she closed her eyes and inhaled his musky scent.

His finger traced her jaw, setting off sparks everywhere he touched. The sensation startled her and she opened her eyes. The heat in his gaze went straight to her already drenched pussy. God, why did doing what was right, feel so bad?

"I wasn't lying on the plane. I've fantasized about you since I was twenty-two, wanted you so bad my teeth hurt. That's all I thought it was, lust. But when I saw you lying on that bathroom floor, bloody and half-conscious, the world fell out from beneath me." He rushed on, "I'm not saying let's get married tomorrow, but soon. You, me, a houseful of kids and a dog. I insist on the dog."

Panic sucked all the air out of the diner. The taste of bittersweet irony filled her mouth. She'd longed to hear those words for as long as she could remember. Now that she had, her only choice was to push him away. She couldn't let her own selfishness hurt another person she loved.

Inhaling a shaking breath, she straightened her spine. *Please God, just let me bluff my way out of this.*

Her mind reeled, searching for something to say. The idea hit her like a lead balloon. Could she do it? She gazed at him, the hope clear in his tired hazel eyes. She had to brazen it out. It was for the best.

God, she wanted to puke.

"Wow, Hank. I don't know what to say." His body tensed and she had to blink back the tears threatening to give her away. "There's no denying

I'm attracted to you, but I'm afraid that's all it is. Lust. We can be fuck buddies."

He grabbed her, forced her to turn and face him in the claustrophobic booth. "Bullshit! What I feel for you is different than lust, and you feel the same."

The truth of his words twisted her heart into a tight knot until she snapped. "You want it all, don't you? The picket fence. The wife and the two-point-five kids. Oh, and let's not forget Fido digging in the yard." Her nails dug into her palms as she forced herself to go on. "Well, Hank, what you want isn't in the cards for me."

"What are you talking about? And don't give me any more of that fuck-buddy crap."

Reaching deep to some well of inner strength she hoped wasn't tapped out, she pushed against his chest. "I need to leave."

He sat still as a statue made of anger and hurt. The only thing that moved was the vein pulsing at his temple. "Not without me."

She'd taken it too far, done too much for this to end any other way than ugly. He wanted her. She wanted him. "And if I said tonight and never again?"

Lowering his lips to hers, he hesitated a breath before they touched. "I'll find a way to convince you otherwise. Before tonight's out, you'll tell me your secret, Beth. Have no doubt."

Chapter Twenty

The kissing lasted through a quick wave goodbye to Chris and Sam, the cab ride to Hank's hotel and most of the elevator ride. Beth didn't come up for air until Hank slipped his room key into the lock, and even then her brain was mired in a lust-induced fog.

Dusk's golden light filtered in through the floor-to-ceiling window, giving the room a soft glow. After what had happened this afternoon, the hotel had given them a suite and moved all of their baggage. Slipping out of her black heels, she felt her feet sink into the plush cream carpet as she sauntered across to the windows and their view of the Spring Mountains. The thick carpet silenced Hank's footsteps, but the quivering sensation dancing along her skin alerted her to his presence a moment before his strong fingers slipped underneath her tacky Vegas hoodie. One foot nudged between hers, forcing them apart until her legs were as wide apart as her shorts allowed.

Reaching around her body, he leisurely lowered the zipper of her hoodie, then pinched both nipples.

Heat seeped into her pussy. The soft cotton came apart as the zipper traveled downward, each centimeter of exposure heightening the anticipation until she moved to yank it off.

"Stop." His growl stopped her in mid-motion. "We have all night, let me enjoy every second of this."

"I don't think I can wait."

"If you can't, I'll have to tie you to the bed to teach you some patience."

"You wouldn't." Her clit throbbed at the idea.

Hank whipped the drapes' braided tie-back cord from its hook and pressed it against the window in front of her face. "Are you sure about that?"

Knees weakening with want, she stilled her fingers.

"Hold this." He thrust the cord into her hand. "A reminder to take it slow."

The rough tie-back scratched against her palm's soft skin, but any thought of it evaporated the second he spread the two sides of her hoodie wider apart. Facing the window, her breasts were exposed to the revelers ten stories below. She doubted anyone could see her, but sill the idea of an audience ratcheted up her desire.

"I can see how hard your nipples are in the reflection. Does this turn you on, Beth? Should I take your shirt all the way off?"

A shiver skittered down her spine. "Yes."

In a flurry of movement, the yellow fabric dropped to the floor. His hands cupped her breasts. "I love your tits. God, they're perfect."

"They're too small."

He nipped at her shoulder. "No. They're just the right size, an ideal handful."

Without warning, he released her and took half a step back. His calloused hands glided down her naked back, stopping just shy of the waistband of her shorts, hanging low on her hips. One firm push had her pressed against the cool glass. The contrast between the air conditioned window and his warm hands spanning her waist transformed her already stiff nipples into diamonds. She grasped the tie back as if it would keep her tethered to reality and save her from the ardor flooding her. His fingers found their way to her elastic waistband and he tugged it downward.

Slowly.

She needed more. Now.

His hazel eyes darkened until they were nearly black. "Stay."

"Why?"

"Please, let me taste my fill." He exhaled a harsh breath. "Not that I think that's possible."

Beth glanced out the window and watched the lights flicker on below her, fighting a battle between the immediate gratification of a fast come and a lasting payoff of a sweaty, toe-curling, exhaustion-inducing orgasm. Then, his soft lips touched the base of her spine, knocking out any thoughts of...well...anything. Electricity shot straight up her spine and down to her core.

He slid the soft material of the shorts down her legs. Hands trailed across the outside of her thighs, Hank's mouth worked across the rise of her ass. Never mind thinking, breathing became an impossibility. She forgot about the people on The Strip below, forgot about Sarah Jane, forgot about being lonely and forgot why she'd ever fought this.

Her breath fogged up the window as she leaned her forehead against the unyielding pane, needing to feel something solid in comparison to her jellified body. He molded her butt, one full globe in each hand, squeezing and teasing. Her clit vibrated and she couldn't hold back the tortured moan from a place inside her consumed by want. Fuck it. She'd had just about enough of foreplay.

In the next heartbeat, his tongue traced a line along the underside of her buttocks and fireworks exploded through her body. Moisture flooded her pussy and she arched her back to give him more of her ass to enjoy. His fingers slipped underneath the soaked cotton center of her panties and plunged two long digits into her quaking pussy. The impact nearly brought her to her knees.

"Oh God, Hank." A plea? A thank you? She had no idea.

He pulled out his fingers to sweep them across her clit, rotating around the tight nub before sinking back inside to press against her G-spot. His left hand snaked up her side until he tweaked her nipple, pulling it taut. The sensual assault continued until the pressure built, higher and higher, pushing her toward infinity. The orgasm undulated within her, a tight explosion with waves of pleasure rolling across her.

Collapsing against the window, Beth gasped for air as the world came back into focus. "That was amazing." She turned to face him. "Thank you."

A lazy half smile curled one side of his mouth as he stood and took a step back. "For what?"

Striding forward, she closed the distance between them. Unable to resist touching him, she brushed the fingers of her non-injured arm down his shirt, still missing a few buttons from their afternoon lovemaking. He was so delicious, so tempting, she craved the taste of him on her lips. But she had to make him understand first.

"Making me see that it was time to let go. My whole life I've held on to things so tightly because I was too scared of letting go and losing everything. I never knew how freeing it was to just be."

"Oh, let's see what else I can do."

Her knees shook at the idea. Making fast work of his few remaining buttons, she stripped away the gray shirt, revealing the muscular chest first honed with two-a-days at football camp that he'd never lost in the years since. Her mouth watered at the sight of his defined abs and hard pecs. The pants fell next, a puddle on the floor in the blink of an eye. The fact he'd gone commando revived the lust momentarily sated by her earlier orgasm.

"You're amazing." She relished his musky smell and ran her fingers down the dark happy trail. The moment she wrapped her hand around the base of his hard cock and stroked, he sucked in a sharp breath.

His hands went to her hair, entwining his fingers with her long brown strands. "Let's call it a tie."

They lowered themselves onto the bed, scattering the overstuffed pillows, and sank into the plush comforter. Ready to explore every inch of him with her hands and tongue, she started at his broad shoulders, then licked her way south to lap at his flat nipples and trace the lines at the top of his six-pack. She stopped right above where his hard-on rested against his stomach and inhaled the warm, musky man scent of him.

Hank. For tonight, her Hank.

Skipping over the obvious target, she smiled at his frustrated groan. When she flattened her tongue and lapped at his balls, the sounds escaping his open mouth morphed into moans of encouragement. Gently, sucking them, she swirled her tongue around them as she once again stroked his straining dick.

"Beth, that feels so fucking good." He squirmed on the bed, forcing her to release his balls.

Not content after how he'd tortured her, she drew his engorged head into her mouth, alternately sucking and licking her prize. Salty and smooth pre-cum covered her tongue like the sweetest nectar. He tasted like heaven. She buried her fingers in her wet pussy and took him in deeper until his cock pushed against the back of her throat. With deliberate care, he pumped in and out of her mouth, his hands holding her head steady. His cock pushed her lips farther apart as she opened to accommodate his girth.

The ache in her pussy couldn't be appeased by her fingers. She needed him inside her, filling her completely. His hands slid from her hair as she rose to her knees and rubbed her hands across her tits. A quick shake of her head and her hair fell in cascades across her shoulders. Spurred on by the desire blazing from his eyes and the lust burning inside her, Beth crawled up his body and lowered herself inch by wet inch onto him. She braced her hands on his stomach and adjusted to his size. Her muscles relaxed and she arched her back so his cock delved deeper. Clit nestled against his pelvic bone, Beth rode him as if she'd been made to do it.

His fingers bit into her hips and he met her every movement with a thrust of his own. "I love you, Beth."

She missed a beat of their shared rhythm and held her breath, waiting for the panic, for the fear to rear up and swamp her. Instead, a new energy spread through her, more powerful than if she'd gobbled a mountain of chocolate-covered espresso beans. Goose bumps dotted her skin and a shiver nearly snapped her spine. Leaning forward, her nipples brushed against the course hair on Hank's chest and she claimed his mouth as only a true lover can.

"I love you, too. Always have. Always will."

Picking up the rhythm again, their bodies, slick with sweat, came together. Hard and soft. Forward and retreat. Always moving toward fulfillment, toward bliss. It started in her toes, the throbbing radiating outward, encompassing her limbs. The orgasm slid up her back, surprising her with its suddenness. Her head snapped back and every muscle in her body locked as lightning flashed and thunder crashed inside her. With one final thrust, Hank came underneath her with a harsh groan.

❧❧❧❧

Hank woke at peace with himself and the world.

Beth curled into his side, her face tucked into the hollow by his shoulder. Her breath came out in a steady rhythm and her eyes were closed, but something in the tension in her shoulders outed her as being awake, her troubled thoughts as obvious as if she spoke them aloud.

Postponing the discussion ahead, he closed his eyes and stroked her silky brown hair, smoothing it off her shoulders in an attempt to soothe her worries away. It had never been like this with Amanda. The future unfolded in his mind's eye, their future, the picture so clear it seemed more memory than imagining. Just the two of them at first, then kids with the Layton hazel eyes and her warm brown skin. Family dinners. Coaching their sons' Pop Warner football teams. Dancing in the living room while the kids slept.

He'd lived a lifetime with Beth before he opened his eyes and admired her naked body stretched out over his.

Perfect.

"Marry me, Beth."

Her body went stiff.

"I mean it. You're everything I want, everything I need."

Tears wet his chest above his heart. "No."

She pulled away from him, rolled over and lowered her legs off the bed. Shoulders shaking, she stayed there, not making a sound.

Blood rushed through his ears and his lungs ached from holding his breath. "Why?"

She didn't move, but flighty energy pulsated off her naked form and he feared she'd disappear if he blinked. The longer she sat unresponsive and silent, the more his confusion built. It grew larger and more demanding until it burned inside him, becoming an inferno of anger.

"What the fuck, Beth, you can't even talk to me now, give me an explanation? This is complete bullshit."

He threw the sheet off and vaulted from the bed. Storming around to her side, he stood, hands on his hips in front of her. Tears spilled down her cheeks but hurt and anger had blocked out any concern.

"Answer me, God dammit. I deserve an answer."

She shook her head. "I can't give it to you."

"Why the fuck not?"

"Because I know you too well, Hank. I know the kind of man you are, how much duty, obligations and promises mean to you. I won't have you feeling obligated to stay with me."

"That makes less sense than a sack of shit."

"I'm sorry." She stood, her body only inches from his. Her hand went up to touch his chest, but she stopped just shy of her goal. "I can't hurt you like I hurt them."

Shuffling, she stepped sideways around him and gathered her clothes piled on the floor in front of the window.

Enough. He marched over to her and yanked the clothes from her grasp. "What are you talking about?"

"The night my parents died. I'd begged them to stop at Denny's on the way home. That's why we were on the road so late. If I hadn't been so intent on my own needs, so selfish, we never would have been hit by the drunk driver. My parents would be alive."

The anger evaporated and he folded Beth into his arms. "You were an eight-year-old girl. You aren't responsible. The other driver is."

"Intellectually I know that, but in my gut... Hank, I watched my mother die, listened to her gasp for breath."

"Darlin', I'm so sorry you went through that and I'd tear the world apart if I could change it."

"I know you would." Her cheek rested against him and she relaxed.

"So help me understand why we can't get married."

She pushed out of his arms, sliding her clothes away from him at the same time, and took a step back. "Because if I married you, I'd be forcing you to sacrifice your dream life for my happiness. I love you too much for that."

"That makes no sense."

Evidence of an internal battle crossed her face in the way her forehead wrinkled and she bit down on her bottom lip. "I had a hysterectomy. No kids. No family. I don't know that I'll ever want to adopt. Maybe God's trying to tell me I'm not meant to have a family."

The hazel-eyed, brown-skinned children he'd imagined playing football with flashed in front of him, then slowly faded away. Of all the things Beth could have said, he'd never expected this. He'd always wanted children of his own, always imagined the next generation of Laytons driving down the streets of Dry Creek, a town his family had helped to found.

While he tried to process the unexpected turn, Beth got dressed. She picked up her purse from the nightstand and turned toward the door.

He snapped out of his daze and chased after her. Gathering her in his arms, he buried his face in her silky hair. "Don't go. It doesn't matter. We don't have to have kids or we can adopt or it can just be us. You *are* meant to have a family. Let me be your family. I love you, Beth."

She turned in his arms, brushing his cheek with her lips. "I love you too, which is why I can't do this. Goodbye, Hank."

His first instinct was to chase, but he'd been doing that for so long now without accomplishing anything but spooking Beth and pressuring her to run.

Paralyzed by hurt, he stood naked next to the bed in which they'd made love and watched her walk out the door.

Chapter Twenty-One

*B*eth cursed her luck.

The flight from Vegas had been fine, but now the turbo jet between Denver and Dry Creek had been grounded with equipment problems. The flight had been canceled. The five-hour drive to Dry Creek would be tedious, but it was better than feeling vulnerable in a strange city. Contemplating the line of fifty people ahead of her at the car rental desk, she wondered if she should just admit defeat, get a hotel room, and rest her throbbing arm.

The crowd emitted a loud groan. A harried clerk slapped down a sign. *No cars available.* In front of her, the line dispersed as people scattered like rats on a sinking ship to other rental car counters where the lines were already dozens of people deep.

She'd give up coffee for a year to have a car right now.

"Need a ride?" Hank jangled a set of rental keys in front of her nose. An easy smile curled his lips, but a sliver of uncertainty shined in his gaze.

Her hard-fought-for composure crumbled in the middle of the airport. With people swarming around them, hurrying from one concourse to another, she stopped trying to move forward and acknowledged the here and now. Here stood the man she loved. Strong. Loyal. Smart. Hot as hell. If she couldn't let go enough to take a chance on him, she was twelve kinds of a fool.

Hank wrapped his arms around her, engulfing her crying form in his warm embrace. "Did you know that I'm going to be the best uncle in the world someday?"

The soft cotton of his Nebraska football polo muffled her chuckle. "Oh, Hank."

"I mean it, Beth. I don't care about some kids we may or may not ever have. I care about you."

"But—"

"We'll take it slow. We don't have to decide everything right away. Trust me." He brushed a kiss across her lips. "Trust yourself."

Looking up into those Layton family hazel eyes, she wanted to say yes but fear had taken up too much room inside her for so long. *You're a real coward, Beth Martinez.* "Hank..."

"I believe in you, Beth. I believe in us. Look, you don't have to say anything this moment, just kiss me."

And she did, with every bit of yes she had in her but couldn't say out loud.

Four and a half hours later, they crossed the Dry Creek County line. The Bighorn Hills loomed up ahead, outlined by the full moon's white light. Named after the bighorn sheep that climbed them, the rounded slopes rose hundreds of feet above the prairie. Dotted with ponderosa pine, prairie grass, jutting outcrops of rocks and scattered patches of sagebrush, the hills seemed spectral set against the bright stars lighting up the night sky.

To tired drivers numbed by the flat monotony of Interstate 80, the Bighorn Hills appeared like mountains in comparison to the never-ending horizontal scenery of the Nebraska plain. For Beth, the sight meant home. And heartbreak.

The memories came unbidden.

The screeching of brakes.

The stench of burning rubber.

Her parents tumbling around the front seat like socks in the dryer.

EMTs pulling her from the wreckage.

"What the hell?" Hank's annoyed tone pulled her back into the present. "That moron is flying."

Beth whipped around in her seat to look out the back window of the tiny subcompact rental car. A truck's high-set headlights zoomed toward them. As it got closer, the driver flashed his high beams, momentarily blinding Beth.

After a few blinks, her sight returned, obscured only by hazy halos that glowed in the middle distance. Her heart rate jacked up as panic buzzed through her body.

Automatically, she tested the seat belt to double-check it was fastened. Her fingers shook as she pulled against Hank's seat belt, making sure he was safe.

Lungs aching with the pressure of holding her breath, she forced herself to inhale and willed herself to think logically. She wasn't eight. She wasn't trapped in the backseat. It wasn't a drunk driver, just someone in a big hurry.

"Slow down and let them pass," she urged. "Maybe it's an emergency."

A vein pulsed in Hank's temple but he didn't say a thing as he eased his foot off the gas pedal.

The truck continued its swift approach, maneuvering at the last moment into the oncoming lane to pass. It pulled alongside, towering over the subcompact.

Nerves taunt, Beth glanced past Hank out the driver's-side window.

Sarah Jane Hunihan sat behind the truck's wheel, her white skin glowing in the moonlight.

Beth couldn't look away as terror spun out of control, hurtling her into a full-on panic.

"Hank!"

ভচভচভচ

Hank forced himself into cop mode, ignoring the instinct to comfort Beth. The truck slammed into the subcompact's driver's side, jostling him in his seat. He punched the gas, shooting the car forward. "Hold on."

The little car gave its all and left the four-by-four in the dust, at least for a moment. The truck swerved behind him, staying on the rental car's tail.

Tires squealed as he sped along the curving road around the bend. The lights of Dry Creek twinkled in the valley below, the deceptive view promising a quick arrival even though they were half an hour out.

It wasn't enough.

Sarah Jane rammed the back of the car, making his head snap forward.

Grasping the steering wheel tighter, he fought to regain control of the car fishtailing on the highway. They had to get away from the truck.

The pitiful rental car engine couldn't outpace a pregnant turtle. He needed to find a side road.

Keeping his gaze locked on the twisting road ahead of them, he pictured a map of Big Horn Hills. There were access roads to the state park dotting the highway, but they weren't well marked. If you didn't know where they were, you'd shoot right past them.

Especially at night.

The truck slammed into the car again, pushing it forward.

"Are we near any of the park access roads?" Tearing his gaze away from the scenery flying past them, Hank glanced at Beth from the corner of his eye.

She sat frozen beside him. Stark terror glistened in her wide-open brown eyes. Her skin had turned ashen.

Gamely, she tried to make eye contact but her gaze skittered back to the headlights glaring at them from the rearview mirror. "Tell me it won't happen again," she demanded in a quiet monotone.

Fuck. Her parents had died on this road, pushed into a ravine by a drunk driver. "Hell no, it won't happen again."

As if to say "oh yeah", the truck slammed into the car once again. The car careened to the left.

He jerked the steering wheel, tires spinning out on the pebbled surface of the highway shoulder. His arms burned from the effort of keeping the rental car tires on the paved highway.

Just as he braced himself for the impact of going off-road, the tires gripped the road and they rushed to the other side.

Yanking the wheel the other way, he fought to keep the car from running off the side of the road.

As the car settled into the right lane, Hank gunned the engine, willing the four-cylinder to run like an eight-cylinder sports car. His gut twisted when the truck appeared once again in his periphery vision. "Beth, you have to concentrate." He fought to keep from yelling and spooking her further. "Is there a park access road nearby?"

The screeching of twisting metal screamed through the night as the truck plowed into them. It took all the power Hank had to keep the little subcompact on the road. "Beth!"

"Yes," she hollered. "Another mile up the road on the left. There's an unmarked ATV path, it's narrow but the car should fit."

"Okay. Keep your eyes peeled and tell me when to turn."

The truck veered into the compact car again. His whole body ached with the effort not to be overwhelmed by the truck's superior force as they barreled side-by-side on the twisting highway.

"Now!"

Jamming his foot onto the brake, his body slammed forward.

The truck passed them.

Revving the tired engine, he steered the car onto the ATV road so narrow, the car barely fit. Bouncing on the deep ruts in the dirt path, there was little Hank could do to avoid the gullies in the road that sent the rental car bounding up into the air.

Pine trees stood guard on both sides, forcing him to stay in the dead center of the road. Still, the pine branches scraped the sides of the car like nails on a chalkboard.

Hank glanced up at the rearview mirror, checking for the truck's headlights. When he returned his gaze to the road, a felled tree lay in the car's crosshairs. His heart threatened to explode in his chest.

Hank smashed down the brakes, a giant cloud of dirt exploding around them. As soon as he came to a stop, he cut the engine and headlights.

Breath shallow, he whipped around to look out the back window as his pulse slowed to a less death-defying speed. Sitting in the dark, silent car, he watched for the truck.

After ten minutes of expecting the worst, he turned to face Beth.

"That was close," she deadpanned in the dark.

His girl was back. Her wry tone made him smile. "Yeah, that's putting it mildly."

"Let's get the hell out of here before she finds us."

"Good plan. Call dispatch and let them know what happened." He flicked the key and the engine sputtered to life. The car chugged into reverse for half a foot before the tires spun, useless in the deep ruts caused by the ATVs that normally owned this access road. "Shit."

"What?" The ringing of her call going through to the sheriff's office blared from her cellphone.

"We're stuck."

"Isn't that—" The dispatcher's voice on the line cut off whatever Beth was about to say.

Beth handed over the phone to Hank, who gave dispatch a quick rundown of Sarah Jane, the attack and their location before snapping the phone shut.

"Okay, we can't stay in the car and be sitting ducks for Sarah Jane. We're going to get close to the road, but stay inside the tree line. Deputies are on their way, but we can't give our location away." He paused, taking in the panicky twitch in her left eye. "You with me? We're going to be alright."

She nodded. "Let's do it."

Even freaked out of her mind, she held her own. If it took the next six decades, he'd make her understand just how much he loved her. Kids or no kids, he didn't give a damn. "Stick close."

They eased out of the car, leaving the doors open to avoid unnecessary noise. Around them the normal night sounds of coyote howls and scurrying nocturnal creatures covered their footsteps. The moonlight filtered through the tree branches, allowing only enough light to see a few feet in front as they made their way through to the road.

Beth stayed close behind him, mimicking his moves and stepping where he did. Swift, but careful, they made their way up a gentle slope.

Straining his ears, he tried to pick out the sound of human footsteps among the rustle of dried leaves. Nothing.

Almost there. The tense muscles in his shoulders unwound.

He could just make out the shiny pebbles on the highway's shoulder when the unmistakable sense of impending danger sent goose bumps marching down his arms.

The Bighorn Hills turned silent, not even a breeze blew.

Halting, he grabbed Beth's arm, pulling her close as he scanned the area. Shadows hid reality. Was that a tree branch or an attacker's arm? Was that the crunch of leaves crushed under a coyote's paw or Sarah Jane's foot? Damn, he wished he had his gun.

After a minute of staring into nothingness, without another sign of an imminent attack, he took a cautious step forward.

So focused on looking out for Sarah Jane, he never noticed the snake hole until it was too late.

His ankle twisted and he tumbled to the ground, pulling Beth down with him. Burning pain shot up his leg and he barely managed to swallow a groan of agony so as to not alert their stalker.

He needn't have worried.

The unmistakable click of a gun being cocked echoed through the brush.

Like a ghost appearing, Sarah Jane stepped out of the shadows, pointing a silver handgun at them. "It's time for you to pay."

Chapter Twenty-Two

*E*ven with her nose buried in the dank dirt and Hank half covering her with his bulk, Beth knew that voice. She'd never heard it raised in anger or whiny with frustration. Not like now, when a tinge of crazy had sharpened the consonants and emphasized the nasal Midwestern twang.

For most of her life, that voice had been a part of her world. She'd sat silent and sweaty under the oak kitchen table to eavesdrop while her abuelita and Sarah Jane drank iced tea and gossiped on hot summer days. When she'd joined Webster and Carter, Sarah Jane had given her the welcome-aboard tour, eased her nerves and warned her about Ed Webster's wandering hands. At the conference in Vegas, they'd chatted about scrapbooking and Sin City's inherent tackiness.

Now, that same voice announced she and Hank were about to die with no more inflection than if she'd said it looked like rain tonight.

Determination to survive stiffened Beth's spine and gave her the courage to face her enemy. Pressing her hands to the cool, hard-packed dirt, she stood up and came eye-to-eye with Sarah Jane's fury.

"How could you let it happen to him?" Her steel-gray bob gleamed in the moonlight and hate blazed from her eyes.

This wasn't what Beth had expected. "What are you talking about? I haven't done anything to anyone."

"Do you know how long it took me to find him? How many hours I stayed in the office searching for him?" Anger shook her voice, took it an octave higher. "Computer records. Personnel files. Wills. Trusts. Looking for clues, any nugget of information. I knew his father wouldn't have let him go far, even after he stole him from my arms."

"Sarah Jane, you need to put the gun down." Hank stood up, his weight heavy on his left leg. "We'll sit down and get everything worked out."

Fear tickled the back of Beth's neck, adding to the frenzied turmoil insider her like a cool breeze on a freezing night. Hank was hurt. He must have twisted his ankle in the fall.

On the verge of freaking out when he sent her a reassuring smile, Beth focused her mind on the immediate danger.

As if he'd never spoken, Sarah Jane went on with her rant, gun trained on Beth. "How could you let him get murdered? It was supposed to be *you*. Wasn't becoming his father's favorite enough for you? Did you have to take his life too?"

"Who are you talking about?"

"Shut up and get down on your knees."

Going after the gun wasn't an option. She'd never get close enough before Sarah Jane got off a shot. Scanning the ground out of the corner of her eye, she looked for weapons. A rock. Big stick. Anything. But the most dangerous thing she found was a trio of dark mushrooms growing at the base of a pine tree. Fuck.

Hands outstretched and right foot barely touching the uneven ground, Hank hobbled forward. "I can only imagine what you've been through. I'm sure once you tell us everything we'll understand. But please, lower the gun."

Sarah Jane's gaze flicked over to him for half a second. Then, with as much care and thought as a person gave to swatting a fly, she fired.

The crack boomed through the trees.

A flurry of beating wings exploded around them while birds took to the sky, escaping the death and fear palpable in the underbrush.

Hank crumbled, blood soaking through his pants near his right knee.

Adrenaline rocketed Beth toward Hank. Forgetting Sarah Jane, the gun and everything except for him, she rushed to his side. The dry October leaves crunched under her knees as she dropped down, taking his head onto her lap.

"Hank." His name tore from her lips, more a desperate cry than anything else.

"Don't worry." He gritted out the words through clenched teeth. "She got my bum knee."

A joke. Her heart was lodged in her throat and he had the gall to make a joke about getting shot. Relief soaked into her bones. "Hank Layton, you're such a pain in the ass."

He smirked up at her. "Is that your way of saying you love me?"

Looking down at the man she'd dreamed about for years, she stopped fighting and opened herself up to the truth. "Yeah, it is."

"You two really make me sick." Bitterness thickened Sarah Jane's voice. "It's not real. Love never is. You know what is though? Revenge. Taking your time, planning everything down to the last bit and then breaking someone into teeny, tiny, jagged pieces."

Heat raced through Beth and she ripped her attention from the man she loved to the woman who threatened him. "How could you do this? Ruin lives for what? Petty revenge?"

"Petty?" She raised her face to the sky and cackled. "No, when someone kills the woman you were and steals your child, petty is not the word for it."

Hank squeezed her hand, slid his cellphone from his back pocket and pushed it into her hand. "Voice record memo," he whispered and struggled into a sitting position against a tree trunk.

Not wanting to draw attention to the phone, she fumbled with it in the shadow until her thumb found the record button on the side. Pay dirt.

"You're under arrest, Sarah Jane Hunihan. You have the right to remain silent..."

As he gave the Miranda warning, understanding blossomed. Backup would be here soon, they needed to keep Sarah Jane talking until then. Recording her confession could be a boon for the prosecution, if the judge ruled it admissible.

"Do you understand these rights?"

"I love your optimism, Sheriff, but I'm not going to jail. Not until I break that bastard."

"Who?" Beth prodded.

"Imagine a young secretary at a big law firm, in love with one of the partners, who's promised to leave his country club wife for her. She becomes pregnant. He swears that if the secretary gives up the baby for adoption, he'll leave his wife. The stupid, naive secretary does it. So what's he do? Ed Webster scrapes her from his life like a piece of gum from the bottom of his shoe."

"That's horrible. I'm so sorry." Hank said.

"I don't need your pity. I didn't then and I don't now. I waited. Watched him. Looked for weakness, all the time searching for my boy. A year ago I found him right here in Dry Creek, an attorney just like his father. Phil had always wondered about his birth parents."

"Phil? Phil Harris was your son?" Shock rippled across her skin.

"I know, not the man I imagined my son would grow up into, but I blame myself. If I hadn't given him up, he would have been stronger, less concerned with revealing himself to his father sooner rather than later. It took me months to convince him that his father wasn't ready and that if he'd just wait a little longer, the timing would be perfect. That timing would have been after I'd crushed him. I didn't have the same outcome when persuading Phil not to worry so much about *your* safety." She leveled the gun at Beth's head. "Poor little Beth Martinez. You were all that stood between me and my revenge. I'd waited so long. I couldn't let someone as insignificant as you stand in my way."

Beth couldn't look away from the gun's barrel as cold fear snaked around her spine. "But I never did anything to you."

"Yes, you did. You wouldn't sell. You took the spotlight from Phil at work. You fucked-up everything." She hurled the words like projectiles. "The plan came to me after I'd found Phil. He let slip that Ed had inside information that the casino would be built on the north end of the Lakota Reservation, near Lake Alice. He'd put up every cent he had to buy the land. I couldn't let him succeed. This was my chance." She paused as if relishing the moment all over again.

"I worked out a very lucrative deal with the Lakota tribe to relocate their new casino off Highway 28 instead. I had every piece of property leading to the reservation tied up. Every one but yours. I had to have yours! I couldn't allow the chance of him even getting one piece!" Her voice had risen to a manic scream. "I wanted him to lose everything. His money. His standing in Dry Creek. I'd make him understand, really understand, what it was like to have an entire community look down on you as ruined goods!"

Off in the distance, the high-pitched blare of police sirens sounded. Just a little longer and help would arrive. Sneaking a peak at Hank's leg, Beth's stomach sank. The splotch of blood soaking through his jeans had grown to encompass his lower thigh, turning his jeans nearly black. His face had paled and his eyelids were nearly closed.

Unaware or unconcerned about Hank's precarious situation, Sarah Jane continued her demented monologue. "I hired those idiots to drug you and kill you. Really, how difficult should it have been? But you managed to survive. And then you got Phil killed. That thug killed him to get to you. Do you know what it's like to lose a son not once, but twice? Do you know what that does to a mother?"

Something inside Beth snapped. "No, I don't— but neither do you. Being a mother isn't about giving birth, it's about caring for someone more than you care about yourself. It's sacrifice. It's love. You're not a mother. You're a monster."

Sarah Jane cocked her head thoughtfully and lowered the gun to her side. "I suppose you're right. I can admit that. But don't you see, Ed Webster is the one who made me into this...monster. He will be punished." She took a step forward. "And so will you."

Beth's stomach twisted and bile rose in her throat. It couldn't end this way, not now. "Please."

"Shut up, girl. First you'll die, and then, after I've ruined him, so will Ed."

Frozen to her spot by indecision, Beth tried to think of an escape as the sirens grew louder. Almost here.

"Fine, if not you then your dear love." Sarah Jane swung the gun toward Hank's slumped figure. "On your knees, or I kill him first."

"No!" She scrambled to her knees, blocking Sarah Jane's shot with her body.

"Ah, the stupid sacrifices we women make for the men we love. Too bad you won't live long enough to learn that they're all out for themselves. Then again, at least you don't have to worry about him leaving you for a newer model."

Flashing red lights lit up the pine trees as patrol cars screeched to a stop on the highway above them.

Doors slammed shut and a deputy shouted clipped orders to the others. The Calvary had arrived, too late for her but hopefully in time for Hank.

Closing her eyes, Beth began to murmur the words she'd heard every day at four p.m. from her abuelita. Her grandmother had dutifully rubbed the worn, dark-blue rosary beads between her arthritic fingers and prayed for the souls of Beth's parents and the unknown drunk driver who'd killed them.

As her dry lips formed the words, a presence warmed the crisp air and she heard abuelita's voice murmur in her ear.

"Hail Mary, full of grace…"

A gunshot silenced her prayer.

Chapter Twenty-Three

$\mathcal{H}$ank ignored the explosive pain throbbing in his knee and fought to remain conscious. His injury wasn't important. Only keeping Beth safe mattered.

Sarah Jane lowered her gun until the angle of the bullet would hit Beth between the eyes. A shot of adrenaline careened through his veins, slammed into his heart and shocked him into full alertness.

Gathering every last bit of energy, he launched himself at Beth.

He wrapped his arms around her kneeling form and flattened her to the ground, morphing himself into a protective shield around her.

A millisecond later a gun fired. His muscles tensed in preparation for impact as everything slowed to a near stop.

A slideshow rolled through his mind. Not of his big accomplishments but of the little things that made life special and whole. The first time he went fishing with his father. His mom's baked macaroni served with a side of lovingly administered nagging. Tossing the football around with his brothers in the empty University of Nebraska football stadium. Teaching Claire to ride a bike.

And when it came to Beth, there were so many memories and, at the same time, not enough. Inhaling, he took in one last whiff of her vanilla perfume that he wished he could enjoy forever. Even if they'd had twelve lifetimes together, it wouldn't have been enough.

It wasn't the children he'd never had that he regretted now. No. In his final moments, Hank mourned the time he could have had with Beth.

But instead of the expected burning lead tearing into his flesh, there was a quiet "umph" and the thump of a body hitting the ground.

Hank looked over his shoulder and the world wobbled as he let go of the air trapped in his lungs.

Sarah Jane lay on her back, her chest jerking up and down in a spastic rhythm. Blood bloomed like a morbid flower on her chest, expanding with each wet, gasping gurgle of breath.

He didn't know which deputy had made the shot, but whoever he or she was, they were about to get a promotion.

Rolling off of Beth, he landed with a thunk on his back. The agony in his leg punched through his adrenaline high.

"Oh my God, Hank!" Beth yanked off her fleece jacket, balled it up and pressed it to his wound.

The pressure made him gasp, but he'd be damned before he'd pass out now. Going for an action-hero vibe, he smirked. "I'll live."

"Is she..." Beth left the word "dead" unsaid, but it hung in the air between them like a sticky spiderweb.

"Not yet." He paused and listened to Sarah Jane's struggle to breathe. "But it doesn't sound good."

The scene in front of Sarah Jane wavered, darkness creeping in on the edges as she fought to stay alive.

So close. She'd been so close to rubbing his face in disgrace and forcing him to confront the wrong he'd committed against her, against them. Her baby Phil. He hadn't grown into the man she would have raised. Yet another sin committed by his father.

A cold numbness seeped into her, shielding her from the pain as blood loss overwhelmed her body's ability to function. The stars, brilliant against the cloudless fall sky, twinkled above her. With all she'd done, she wouldn't be going in that direction. Her soul would sink into the ground, heating as she fell deeper and deeper into the hell below.

Salvation was for the living, and in her heart, she'd stopped living that night twenty-eight years ago. The truth crystallized in her mind, shattering her anger. Stunted with hurt and resentment, she'd surrendered to the black void without ever realizing it.

"I did what I had to do." Pain slurred her quiet words.

In an instant, Beth appeared above her and kicked the gun from her hand, not that there was any need. Sarah Jane barely had the strength to form words, let alone curl her fingers around the trigger.

Beth's heart-shaped face hovered in the center of her ever-darkening field of vision.

Then, the light disappeared.

There were no angels. No sweet face of God.

Eternity spread out in every direction like a heavy quilt smothering her on a hot summer night.

Deputies swarmed around Beth as she tried to process what had just happened.

Her grandparents' house.

The threats.

The vandalism.

The goons in Vegas.

Phil dying in front of her eyes.

Hank being shot.

All of it because of Sarah Jane's hunger for revenge.

Unable to make sense of the truth, she wrapped herself in an icy detachment and distanced herself from the death and misery surrounding her. Lost in a wispy cloud of numbness, she continued to kneel by Sarah Jane's body. A breeze teased her hair, lifting the ends until the strands tickled her cheeks.

"Excuse me, ma'am, the paramedics want to check you out." A deputy loomed over her, holding out a hand.

Startled out of her daze, Beth shook off her protective mental gauze and emerged back into reality. She grasped the deputy's wide hand and pulled herself up, taking stock of the chaos.

Paramedics toting heavy duffel bags swarmed Hank and cut away the bloody mess of his jeans. Even from ten feet away, his knee looked like a mangled mess of shredded muscle, shattered bone and blood. Fighting back the worry-induced nausea, she brushed past the deputy and rushed over.

"Will he be okay?" She squatted down next to him.

The paramedic stayed focused on Hank's injury. "Looks like the bullet missed any major arteries." He zipped up his duffel and stood. "Be right back with the stretcher."

He loped through the trees and toward the highway at an easy, steady pace.

"Thank God you're alright." If she hadn't already been kneeling, relief would have knocked her to the ground. She sent up a quick prayer for Hank, for her, for everything.

"It takes more than a crazy lady to take me out." Hank's large hand engulfed hers. "You have to remember the women in my family. I've had advanced training."

Humoring him more than anything else, she smiled at his joke. But the truth was they both would have died if his deputies hadn't arrived in time.

Her entire life she'd tried to encase herself in a protective bubble with the same single-minded conviction Sarah Jane had depended on for her plans of revenge. In the end, it had blown up in both their faces and she'd almost lost the only man she'd ever loved.

Lowering her face, she brushed her lips across his in a brief kiss of hope, of new beginnings.

"It's all over, Beth," he murmured. "Everything will go back to normal."

"But I don't want that. I want more." Certainty struck her like a lightning bolt. "There are so many things I've missed out on and left undone. All because I was scared."

He squeezed her hand. "Of what?"

"I was scared of putting myself out there, losing someone or something else. I went into estate law because it was low pressure. I loved the mental chess of being a trial attorney, but the risks were so high..."

Chest tight and throat raw, she stopped to swallow back the tears threatening to overflow onto her cheeks. Her abuelita had warned her all those years ago, but she hadn't understood. She'd been a scared eight-year-old with a broken spirit hiding in her bedroom. The bed had creaked in protest when her grandmother had sat down. She'd wrapped Beth inside her warm embrace and kissed the top of her head. "God doesn't give you your family," she'd whispered, "he gives you the strength and courage to make your own."

For so long, she'd walked the wrong path, but not anymore.

"I thought by regulating everything in my life, I was keeping myself safe, insulating myself. I never let go." An unsure smile turned her lips upward. "Not until you."

Hank contemplated her, saying nothing after her declaration. As the silence grew, a nervous energy fizzed along her skin and jumbled her stomach. Then a smile crinkled the corners of his eyes. All of the tension whooshed out.

"I love you, Beth Martinez. When we get out of here, there's an Elvis impersonator I'm taking you to meet."

"I have no idea what that means," she laughed. "But I love you too. Always have. Always will."

Chapter Twenty-Four

Beth's nose twitched and the impending sneeze built until she couldn't hold it back any longer. The release sent a small cloud of dust up from the bookshelf where she'd plucked her parents' wedding photo. Pivoting, she turned back toward the cardboard box on her walnut desk and dropped it in with the rest of her knickknacks.

"Bless you." Ed Webster stood in the doorway of her office at Webster and Carter.

In the three months since she'd last set foot in the law firm, he'd lost weight. His cheekbones stood out in gaunt relief from the rest of his face and dark circles had taken up permanent residence under his eyes.

"I haven't hired a new cleaning person since the last one quit. Sarah Jane would have taken care of it, and now..." He let his words die off and shoved his hands in his pockets.

Tempted as she was to tell him to go to hell, she'd known when Hank dropped her off this morning that her former mentor wouldn't let her leave today without the talk.

"Come on in, Ed."

Like a stray dog thankful for any scrap of affection, his face lit up and he hurried to an empty chair. "So, I can't change your mind?"

"I needed a change." Switching over to family advocacy law had been huge challenge, but she loved her new life. She'd never been happier.

"Yeah, I've gotten that from a lot of folks ever since...well, ever since it came out."

That was small-town justice for you. Word had spread like wildfire and censure swept in behind, turning his bumper crop of a life into a fallow field. "I heard about the divorce. Sorry."

He shrugged, his once beefy frame shrunken to skeletal proportions. "To be expected, I guess. She'd always suspected there were others, but public confirmation was too much. This practice is all I have left and the bank is breathing down my neck, wanting the balloon payment for the loan I took to finance the land purchases, so I probably won't have it for much longer."

Beth could only imagine what it had been like for him. She'd lived under a microscope. Conversations had slammed to a stop whenever she'd rolled her cart into a new aisle at the grocery store, picked out Christmas presents at the mall or walked into the New Year's Eve party at the country club. Dry Creek's gossips had rolled the situation around and examined it from every angle. No one had escaped scrutiny—including Ed's and Sarah Jane's son, Phil.

"You know it's not true. Not that I can stop the talk. Not that anyone would believe me."

He had to be kidding. "Don't bother. Sarah Jane told me everything. You may not deserve all the hell you're getting, but you're not the injured party here."

"I was a different man then, drank too much and hurt people without a second thought. I was an asshole, probably still am, but nothing like that. When Sarah Jane lost the baby—"

"Lost the baby?" She reined in the urge to slap him. "You make it sound like Phil wandered off from the hospital. The newspaper got ahold of the police reports. They found her diaries, almost thirty years' worth of written misery. She gave the baby up for adoption in a pathetic attempt to hold on to *you*."

"I haven't read the paper in months. Shit, is that really what she wrote? I knew she'd been confused, but I hadn't realized she'd totally lost touch with reality."

"What are you talking about?"

"Phil isn't our son."

Before her eyes, Ed deflated. His face changed from haggard to haunted. His hands shook as he stared off into the distance.

"Right before I broke up with her, we went to Denver for the weekend for a client meeting. She was six months pregnant, but no one knew. She'd worked so hard at hiding it under bulky clothes. I was panicking, worried my wife would find out. I'd tried to convince her to give the baby up, but she wouldn't."

His voice trembled and he blinked several times before continuing.

"The cramps started at the hotel. She'd taken a bath, hoping they'd go away. I'd gone down to the hotel bar to mellow out with a couple of bourbons. When I got back to the room two hours later, she was still in the tub. The blood...it was everywhere. They saved her, but the baby didn't make it."

He didn't bother to wipe away the tears spilling onto his cheeks. "The whole time, I'd been wishing that baby would disappear. You'd think I would have been thrilled. A nurse came and took me to say goodbye in the morgue. They'd cleaned him up, wiped away the blood and wrapped him in a blue-and-white striped blanket. Hell, he was so tiny, shorter than my forearm, with these little fingers that should have curled around mine."

Beth sank down in her chair and Ed wept in front of her, silently.

"I knew she didn't believe me or the hospital folks when she woke up without a baby. Nothing we said could convince her. They'd already cremated the baby. It was like he'd never existed." Ed's voice broke and he gulped in air like a condemned man. "And damn my soul to hell, that's how I acted. Like it had never happened. Any time she brought it up I ignored her, until finally she made herself believe she'd given up the baby. I figured if it made my life easier for her to say that, then fine, I'd play along. But I never realized she really believed it."

Nausea rolled over Beth in waves as she gripped the arms of her desk chair, willing her stomach to relax. She wanted to scream "liar" at him, make him take it all back.

But his story answered one of the largest doubts about Sarah Jane. Finding her long-lost son in the office where she worked seemed a little too convenient. And how had she known it was Phil? Nearly thirty years ago, adoption cases were considered closed. Even if both the child and the birth parent wanted to find each other, the hurdles were extraordinary.

The chance of Sarah Jane finding her son was astronomical. Her diaries had never detailed how she'd discovered what she believed to be the truth. Instead, she'd written about the curl of Phil's smile and the way he talked with his hands, so much like his father that she just knew it was him.

"How could you have done this? People died because of you two and your twisted, fucked-up secrets."

He sank farther into his seat, as if he could disappear into its leather cushions. "I never meant—"

"No, I'm sure you never did. You never meant to be an asshole. It was because you drank too much. You never meant to cheat on your wife. It was because the others were so willing. You never meant to wreck a woman's psyche so thoroughly that she lost touch with reality and devoted her life to ruining yours. You don't mean to do a lot of things, Ed, but everything sure seems to go to shit around you." She rocketed out of her seat, snatched the box from the desk and stormed to the door.

"I loved her once. I really did."

The bittersweet vibrato in his voice stopped her cold. She couldn't help but turn to take one last look at the man who'd unthinkingly hurt so many lives.

Ed still sat in the chair, facing away from her, a silhouette in the winter's late-afternoon sunset spilling in from the window.

For most of her career he'd loomed large, dominating the conversation and tone in every boardroom he entered with just his presence. Now, he sat alone in a fast-darkening room, eclipsed by the light of truth streaming down on him.

Nothing she could say would bring him any lower than he'd brought himself. Her new life started the moment she walked out the front door into the arms of the man she loved.

Without uttering a word, she turned and walked into the cold January sunshine.

Chapter Twenty-Five

Beth blew some warmth onto her freezing hands. Early January in Nebraska would never be confused for a tropical island paradise. The frost-covered ground crunched under her boots when she stepped down from her grandparents' front porch to the hard dirt below and hustled to the crowd of people gathering on the driveway. What she wouldn't do for a cup of steaming coffee.

An arm wrapped around her waist and pulled her backwards until she fit snuggly against a hard body—one that had kept her up way too late last night. Hank brushed his lips across the nape of her neck above her coat collar and her formerly frozen insides melted.

"Looks like you could use this." Like manna from heaven, a bee-decorated coffee mug appeared in front of her.

"Just when I thought I couldn't love you any more." She swiped the mug from him and sipped the piping-hot brew. Mocha with a shot of caramel. Yep, he was a keeper.

"You sure you want to do this?"

Looking around at her neighbors and friends stomping their feet to keep warm in the bitter cold, she considered calling it all off. Going ahead would change everything. Her shoulders twitched with a shiver of apprehension. After all that had happened, not one person would think any worse of her. But she would. She'd worked too hard during the past few months to go back to her old ways.

"Yeah, I'm sure."

"Ms. Martinez, I need you to sign a couple of documents real quick and then we can get started." Frank Eastwick of Eastwick Auctioneers motioned her over to his truck and the battered briefcase resting on its hood.

"Be right there." Nervous energy took her voice up an octave.

Stepping out of Hank's embrace, she turned to face him. Gone was the vacation beard and the knee brace he'd had to wear after surgery. Bundled up in a bright-red parka with a white capital N embroidered across the back, he fit in perfectly with the rest of the state, breathlessly waiting for the championship college football game. Something ornery that had nothing to do with football twinkled in his hazel eyes.

"You can't go until I get payment for that coffee." He pulled her close and lowered his head until their lips were only inches apart.

In an instant, her nipples hardened and butterflies started doing cartwheels in her stomach. "That was a gift." She raised her head, cutting the distance between their mouths to mere millimeters. "There is no payment for gifts."

"Wanna bet?"

The kiss curled her toes. Suddenly, January turned unseasonably warm and balmy under the tight confines of her wool coat.

"What is it with my children? Where did I go wrong?" Glenda Layton's indignant questions cut through the lust fogging her brain.

Hank ended the kiss. "Hi, Mom."

"You are in public, you know." Never one for the cold, the only part of Glenda visible was her brown eyes above the neon-green scarf wrapped around her neck and face. Her matching green down coat reached her knees. The entire outfit was topped off with a white ski cap that she'd managed to bedazzle with neon-green stones. "If it wasn't for this godforsaken cold, Bob and I would sell the RV just so we could keep an eye on you kids. First Claire and now you, getting frisky at inappropriate times. It's like I raised free-love hippies or something."

"Yep, we're planning on turning Dry Creek into a nude commune. I'm going to ditch the whole sheriff gig to grow pot."

Glenda harrumphed and rolled her eyes. "Nobody likes a smart mouth."

Hank dropped a quick peck on his mother's wool cap. "Only you, Mom."

Her eyes crinkled at the corners, a telltale sign she smiled under the neon-green scarf.

Biting back her own smile at the normal state of affairs between Glenda and Hank, Beth took a step away from his warmth. "I have to sign some papers. Be right back."

ꙮꙮꙮ

Hank admired the sway of Beth's hips as she made her way to the auctioneer's truck. "Okay, so what was that show all about, Mom?"

She shrugged her neon-covered shoulders. "I don't know what you're talking about."

Like hell. If the government ever needed a sixty-something covert agent experienced in interrogation and subterfuge, Glenda Layton was their woman. "Mom."

"Oh alright. I need to know who that tall girl is over there with the platinum-blonde hair. She has tattoos, four of them that I can see."

He scanned the crowd for his mom's target. It didn't take long to spot her. About five feet, eleven inches, wearing painted-on jeans and a black leather jacket, she had short blonde, almost white hair. Saying she stood out was putting it mildly.

"You can only see her skin from the neck up, how did you see any tattoos?"

"You can't see them now. I've been watching her for the past week."

Poor girl. If she'd landed on Glenda's radar, she was in for a world of trouble. "So what has you so curious about her?"

"I've spotted her arguing with Sam." Glenda lowered her voice. "Twice."

What in the hell was his by-the-book brother doing going toe-to-toe with a wild child? Oh, this was going to be good. "Why don't you just ask Sam then?"

Glenda shot him an are-you-stupid look. "You think I haven't? That boy is tighter than a clam when it comes to his business. I'm his mother. Why he thinks he has to keep secrets from me, I'll never know."

At that moment, the Layton in question got out of his Volvo sedan. Standing stick straight, Sam surveyed the crowd. A devious smile curled his lips the moment he locked eyes on the tall blonde and he threaded through the crowd toward her.

Interesting. Very interesting.

Beth made her way to Hank's side just as the auctioneer stepped to the front porch.

Frank turned on the microphone and inhaled a deep breath. "Remember folks, all proceeds of this auction go to the Dry Creek County Big Brothers and Big Sisters Program. We'll start the bidding at…"

Beth slipped her hand into Hank's. "Come on, let's go."

"Don't you want to stay?"

Glancing back at the people milling around her grandparents' front yard, she remembered the birthday parties out back, the way her abuelita's cheese enchiladas smelled and the many nights she'd spent as a teenager, tucked away on a lumpy twin mattress dreaming about Hank Layton. The memories were hers forever. She took them with her wherever she went.

"That's just a house." She brushed his lips with hers. "You're my home."

A Note From Avery

Hey you!

I really hope you enjoyed Hank and Beth! They get me right in the feels. If you have a second to leave a review of Dangerous Flirt, that would be awesome! And if you're want to know what happens between Sam and the tattooed Josie, check out Dangerous Tease.

Please stay in touch (avery@averyflynn.com), I love hearing from readers! Want to get all the latest book news? Subscribe to my newsletter for book gossip, monthly prizes and more!

And don't forget to check out the other Layton books: Dangerous Kiss and Dangerous Tease.

xoxo,

Avery

Books By Avery Flynn

The Killer Style Series
High-Heeled Wonder (Killer Style 1)
This Year's Black (Killer Style 2)
Make Me Up (Killer Style 3)

Sweet Salvation Brewery Series
Enemies on Tap (Sweet Salvation Brewery 1)
Hollywood on Tap (Sweet Salvation Brewery 2)
Trouble on Tap (Sweet Salvation Brewery 3)

Dangerous Love Series
Dangerous Kiss (Laytons 1)
Dangerous Flirt (Laytons 2)
Dangerous Tease (Laytons 3)

Novellas
Hot Dare
Betting the Billionaire
Jax and the Beanstalk Zombies (Fairy True 1)
Big Bad Red (Fairy True 2)

Newsletter

Subscribe to Avery's newsletter for news about her latest releases, giveaways and more!

Street Team

Join the Flynnbots and get sneak peeks at Avery's latest books and more!

Visit Avery's website at www.averyflynn.com

Facebook: https://www.facebook.com/AveryFlynnAuthor

TSU: https://www.tsu.co/AveryFlynn

Pinterest: https://www.pinterest.com/averyflynnbooks/

Twitter: https://twitter.com/averyflynn

E-mail: avery@averyflynn.com